Anna spotted Daniel behind the locked glass door.

Oh Lord, please help me reach him!

She glanced over her shoulder. Ted hung back, midway on the staircase, out of Daniel's view.

"Better find a way to get out of this, Anna." Ted's voice carried a clear threat. What had happened to him?

Anna walked slowly toward Daniel, praying away the threat of Ted's menacing presence behind her. The thudding of Ted's footfalls on the stairs filled her ears, closing in on her. Anna stopped.

Daniel's eyes flashed to a spot above her, his smile disappeared. He jiggled the knob, causing the glass panes to rattle in their frames.

"You can still get out of this." Ted's words grated between clenched teeth. The fake smile in his voice chilled her.

Fear kept her feet planted to the floor. *Move!* She sucked in a breath and walked forward. The walls seemed to grow narrower, squeezing the breath out of her.

Daniel rattled the knob again.

NANCY TOBACK has two adult children, a teenage son, and one grandson. Nancy was born and raised in Manhattan and now resides in Florida. If there's spare time after being wife, mother, and writer, Nancy is a watercolorist and charcoal artist, and she enjoys gourmet cooking. You may e-mail her at backtonan@aol.com.

Books by Nancy Toback

HEARTSONG PRESENTS
HP581—Love Online (with Kristin Billerbeck)

Anna's
Journey

Nancy Toback

Heartsong Presents

In loving memory of my precious mother, Ann. Your unconditional love and support meant everything to me. And to my little sister, Annette. I think of you both every single day, and I miss you with all my heart. Waiting to meet up with you on the other side of the Jordan.

A note from the Author:
I love to hear from my readers! You may correspond with me by writing:

Nancy Toback
Author Relations
PO Box 721
Uhrichsville, OH 44683

ISBN 1-59789-130-4

ANNA'S JOURNEY

Our mission is to publish and distribute inspirational products offering exceptional value and biblical encouragement to the masses.

PRINTED IN THE U.S.A.

one

Anna McCort dashed across Second Avenue to the Manhattan tune of blaring horns and cabbie expletives. Truck exhaust blasted her legs. Diesel fumes invaded her sinuses. She forged through the black vapors and hopped up on the curb.

She would soon be out of this crazy city. Anna grimaced. She'd wasted a year of her life here. Still, she had no one to blame but herself.

She drew a deep breath and tipped back her head. The sun shone in a smog-free October sky as though the city beckoned her to stay.

Too little, too late—like Ted's marriage proposal.

A spurt of anger gave her impetus. Anna bulldozed her way to the corner diner through the stampede of pedestrians. She pulled open the heavy glass door and surveyed the crowded room in search of Jane.

No Jane.

That was Jane—lovable, unreliable Jane.

Anna glanced toward the counter where the owner stood in a bacon-grease cloud, his arms crossed over his chest like a genie reluctant to grant wishes. She waved to catch his attention and managed a weak smile. "Stavros, may I please have that booth?" She pointed to the corner of the room.

His bushy brows drew together, deepening his permanent scowl.

"I know the rule." Anna kept her smile in place. "Two or more to a booth, but I'm expecting someone."

Stavros eyed her warily then gave a curt nod.

"Thanks." Anna hastened to the table, lowered herself into the seat, and ordered a carafe of coffee from a passing waitress. She pulled her sweater sleeves to her knuckles and stared past her reflection in the glass window. She pressed her fingers to her burning eyes—the aftermath of three days spent crying over Ted. Why she'd wasted tears on him, though, was beyond her comprehension.

The bell on the door jangled, drawing her attention toward the front. *Still no Jane.* Anna glanced away, and her gaze locked with the man's in the booth in front of hers. The handsome stranger smiled and raised his glass of juice in a toast. His female companion chatted away, appearing as blissfully unaware of his flirtatious behavior as Anna had been of Ted's.

Anna jerked her gaze back to the window. *Cheat!* Even when she'd confronted Ted with the hard evidence, he rocked heel-to-toe, hands in his pockets. His crafty blue eyes shifted as he tried to form an alibi. *I wasn't really cheating on you. It's not like we've been intimate.* The memory made her blood pump lava all over again. How dare he try to place the blame on her because of her beliefs?

"Yoo-hoo!"

Anna swiped the anger off her face and gave Jane a wave. She watched her cross the room, Jane's blond hair wind-tangled and a blazer hanging off one shoulder. *She looks like she's just run a marathon.*

"Whew!" Jane slipped into the booth and dropped her purse on the seat. "Sorry I'm late, but I missed one bus and had to catch a cab at—"

"That's okay, I'm just glad to see you." She poured Jane coffee from the carafe then stiffened. The man in the next booth sat with his chin resting on his hand, openly observing them. A Don Juan? Or did she know him? He looked sort of familiar. Anna set down the pot and turned her attention back to her frazzled friend.

"Thanks." Jane peeled the top from a creamer. "Okay." She grimaced. "What's so important that you couldn't tell me over the phone?"

The initial pain of the breakup—the reason she'd called Jane for a face-to-face—had subsided to a dull ache. Now she'd have to go over the incident in public. Anna shifted in her seat. "It's about Ted. He, um, he. . ." She quickly switched her gaze to the approaching waitress.

"What'll it be, girls?" The woman retrieved a pencil from somewhere in her black beehive hairdo.

Grateful for the interruption, Anna gave the server her full attention. "Scrambled eggs and rye toast please." .

"Ditto," Jane said. She leaned forward. "Go on, Ted what?"

The breakup was Ted's fault, so why did she feel the fool? Anna gave a mild shrug. "It's over between us."

Jane slapped her palm on the table. "What? Are you telling me you and Ted broke up?"

"Shh." Anna's gaze darted to the stranger in the next booth. She distinctly saw awareness flicker in his dark eyes. "He proposed first."

"*Proposed?*" Jane squinted. "Help me out here. I thought you wanted the white-picket-fence thing."

White teeth flashed against olive skin as Don Juan spoke to his companion. Anna inched down in the booth, using Jane's head to block her view of him. "He proposed *after* I found out he was cheating." She whispered, hoping Jane would take the hint and lower her voice.

"Oh, Anna, I'm so sorry. What happened?"

Jane's face bore no surprise. Anna took a swallow of coffee, dejection washing over her. She stared down at her cup and relayed the basics of the confrontation, feigning more irritation than hurt.

"In the end, Ted blamed me. He said if it hadn't been for my 'old-fashioned morals' he wouldn't—"

"Oh, please! That is just so typical of Ted." Jane leaned in closer. "Besides being a control freak, Ted's got what we psychologists call character disorder."

Anna chuckled in spite of herself. "What do you mean?"

"Ted never assumes responsibility for his behavior. It's always the other guy's fault."

She was tempted to commiserate, but truth was truth even when it hurt deep down inside. "Not in this case. I'm the one who followed Ted to New York, believing in happy-ever-after."

Anna pressed her fingers to her throbbing temples, clinging to one consolation. The Lord had kept a door open. Aunt Mary had responded to her e-mail, welcoming Anna with open arms whenever she was ready to join her at the orphanage in Haiti. Satisfaction flickered through her gloom.

"What's that smile about?" Jane scanned her face with a knowing gaze.

"Nothing." She wasn't up to discussing her plans in a diner. And as much as she appreciated Jane, her advice would only add to the voices already chattering in her head, urging her to be normal. No one could persuade her to abandon God's call to work with children. Not this time. Not ever again. She had let Ted sidetrack her, and look what that got her. A knife straight to her heart!

Jane's shrug belied the curiosity in her eyes. "Bottom line, Anna; you were too good for Ted."

"Right—I know." Still, Ted had been her first and only boyfriend. "For the record, Ted would disagree with you. He liked to remind me that men didn't line up at my door." Her short laugh rang hollow in her own ears. "Like I was lucky to have him."

The sadness in Jane's eyes made her regret her pitiful confession.

"You know better, don't you? There's a man out there who'll love you to pieces."

Anna buried her doubts under a smile. "I wish I'd ended it with Ted before it started, instead of trying to prove I wasn't the McCort family oddball."

Jane sighed. "Talk about inferiority complexes, Anna. You're a perfect example." She reached across the table and squeezed her wrist. "I know you loved the guy but, I'm sorry, for the life of me I can't figure out why."

Anna swallowed around the lump forming in her throat.

"Thanks. My emotions swing between hurt and anger, but I'll be fine." She fiddled with a sugar packet, unable to stop her hands from trembling. "Anyway, Ted changed so much in the past year. He's not the same man I fell in love with."

Jane let out an unladylike snort. "*You* may think he changed, but to me he's the same Ted we knew in college."

The waitress arrived and plunked down their plates with a clatter. Anna's appetite shriveled, but she laced her fingers and prayed silently.

"I'm starved." Jane salted her eggs and speared them with a fork. "When did all this happen?"

Anna edged her dish away, studying the scarred table as the painful memories flooded back. The only good to come of the breakup was that it set her back on course. "Wednesday."

"Humph! Some best friend you are." Jane's mouth turned down in a pout. "You waited three days to tell me?"

I did tell my best friend. Anna's gaze lingered on Jane in sad wonderment. How did Jane, or anybody, make it through life without the Lord's help? "I needed time to be alone with God."

Jane inspected her coffee mug. "I see."

The comment was less than convincing, but she'd continue to pray, believing Jane would some day come to know God's love.

Anna looked up, unable to resist a glance at the stranger. He was looking at her with something like approval in his eyes. She quickly refocused on Jane and watched her spread jelly on her toast.

"I had my suspicions about Ted for a while, Anna. He hinted he was none too happy about the celibacy thing."

Anna's stomach lurched. She opened her mouth to speak.

Jane held up her hand. "Listen, I admire you for having stood by your Christian convictions, but—"

"Why didn't you warn me? I would've warned you had it been the other way around."

Jane sat up straighter, eyes wide. "It was only a suspicion, and would you have listened?"

Anna's heart sank, but she lifted her chin a notch. "Well, I don't care anymore." Had everybody known, making her all the more a fool? "In my heart of hearts, I always knew I wasn't Ted's missing rib."

"Missing *what*. . .?" Jane rolled her eyes in dawning. "Anna, please, not the Adam and Eve story again. What are you planning to do? Check under a guy's shirt before you date him?"

Despite her battered emotions, Anna relinquished a smile. Jane *was* funny. And she was intentionally being flip. For all Anna's best efforts at bravado, Jane most likely knew tears were a heartbeat away.

"Missing ribs," Jane muttered. "What a criteria."

Anna's heart sank another notch. Perhaps her dreams had been far-fetched. She forked the cold eggs around her plate.

"Have you phoned your folks yet?"

"Yes." Anna set down her fork, abandoning the effort to eat. "And my mom rattled off names of bachelors in town—'if only I'd come home.' "

"To Akron?" Jane dipped her chin. "Things can't be *that* bad."

"Stop making fun of Akron."

"I'm not. I'm making fun of *you*." Jane laughed. "You still wear clothes two sizes too big, but living in Manhattan has done wonders for you. At least you're not the fraidy cat who tiptoed into the dorm room and—"

"All right, enough." Anna's gaze skittered to the dark-haired stranger. He was undoing the top button of his shirt. Apparently, she wasn't the only one feeling the heat rise as people packed the diner. She narrowed her eyes. He did look familiar.

"A religious fraidy cat, to boot," Jane added.

Anna tried to shrug off the remark, hoping she'd grown spiritually since her college days. She had learned one critical truth from dating Ted: She couldn't force her beliefs on anyone. She sighed and snapped off a piece of toast. "Was I that bad?" Why ask? Her own brother and sister had tagged her as Miss Goody-Two-Shoes.

"Hmm, let me think." Jane batted her lashes. "Allison and

I would sit in the dorm discussing how rich and famous we'd become, and you'd turn the TV to a channel about hungry children."

"Hint, hint, huh?" Anna shrugged, but a doomsday feeling settled on her heart. She'd been a horrid example to Jane. "I hope you know I was serious about working at the orphanage after graduation. It's just that I put Ted ahead of God's plans for my life."

Jane waved away her confession. "You're being too hard on yourself. Ted knew you as a friend first. He knew which buttons to push." The reminder made Anna's chest tighten. "I tried to warn you when Ted showed up at campus Bible studies that he had an agenda."

Anna found herself eyeing the handsome stranger again. He nodded at his companion then slanted a glance at Anna for a brief moment. That sense of recognition flickered again.

Jane tapped the table. "Are you listening to me?"

Anna looked away from him with effort. "Of course."

"You did nothing wrong. You just like to think the best of people." Jane popped her gaze around the room. "It's an admirable quality but slightly dangerous in this town."

Anna gave a choked laugh, fighting to not spill her emotions. How foolish to have fallen prey to the first man who'd shown her an interest. From now on, she'd keep her emotions in check. "I guess I was naive."

"*Was?*" Jane snorted. "You're on another planet when it comes to men."

In her peripheral vision, Anna couldn't help but notice the stranger rise from his seat. She chose to ignore the disappointment dipping in her stomach. She still couldn't recall where she'd seen him. Now she probably never would.

Jane cleared her throat. "Earth to Anna."

"Yes, I'm kissing. I mean, *listening!*"

Jane honked out a laugh. "What do you know? A Freudian slip! I just love those. Makes me think you're gonna be all right after all."

Anna gulped the remainder of her coffee. She should've stayed holed up at home longer. What insanity had caused her to make such a stupid mistake?

"Why are we still sitting here?" Jane shoved her plate away and motioned the waitress to the table. "Check, please."

The woman bounded over. "No check." She gave a conspiratorial wink with eyes ringed in heavy black pencil. "Some guy already paid."

two

"Some guy?" Jane scanned the room. "What guy?" She turned her suspicious eyes on Anna, one brow arched.

"I have no idea." The heat of a blush inched up her neck. "But we can't accept."

The waitress pointed to the register. "That's him cashing out. Wish I was twenty years younger," she mumbled as she strode away.

Anna glanced up with what she hoped was a look of surprise and summoned a polite smile. The man's companion slipped out the door.

"Who is he?" Jane's gaze traveled from the man back to Anna. "Do you know the guy?"

"Absolutely not."

Jane smirked. "So why do you look so guilty?" She gave him a wave. "Thank you," she mouthed, though he stood only a short distance away.

"My pleasure." His dark eyes shifted and lingered on Anna. Her heart drummed harder in her ears. She should've figured a silky voice would complete the picture.

"What's your name?" Jane's boldness made Anna cringe and garnered looks from other diners. If only she could disappear under the table.

"Daniel." Smiling, he turned back to the cashier.

Jane sucked in a breath. "Now *that* is a sight to behold." Her gaze scanned him head to toe. "I like the look. . .jeans and a white dress shirt. An urban cowboy of sorts."

Anna lifted her shoulder in a mild shrug. "Yeah, I guess."

"You guess?" Jane eyed him on his way out the door. "It's me you're talking to. He's got that unshaven-for-a-day look you always told me you loved. He's just your type. Admit it."

Anna squelched her excitement at his show of interest. She wouldn't allow anything to set her off course—including a shadowed jawline. "Not that it matters to me." She slipped a tip under the coffeepot. "In a city of millions, I'll never run into him again." *And thankfully so.* If Ted had ripped her heart to shreds, imagine what *Daniel* could do to a woman's heart! Goose bumps skittered up her arms.

"Too bad he didn't approach you." Grinning, Jane ignored her cool show of disinterest. "You might want to do some rib checking."

☙

Anna sat on her four-poster bed and ran her hand down the carved bedpost. Her mother had the family heirloom shipped to her as a surprise. She'd have to ship it back soon. She wouldn't be the next married McCort, proving her family right; she was doomed to follow in the footsteps of Aunt Mary, who "couldn't find a husband if her life depended on it."

Anna closed her eyes and sighed. When she was growing up in Ohio, her mother resented her frequent visits to her aunt's church. However, her parents worked long hours, and Anna, being the youngest, wasn't permitted outdoors alone. When she tried to get her older brother and sister to play, they let her know subtlety she was a bothersome tagalong.

But the honk of Aunt Mary's car horn had been music to her ears. She would abandon her storybooks, dash out the door, and hop into her aunt's rusty convertible for the bumpy ride to the storefront church where people talked about God a lot and made her feel special.

Anna lifted her Bible from the nightstand and ran her fingers over the worn cover. When she turned sixteen, it was the members of Community Church who'd thrown her a party. Instead of being grateful, her mother warned afterwards that Anna was hiding in church.

Hiding? She had tried it her mom's way, but Ted's love couldn't compare with the unconditional love she'd felt from God and the foster children at her aunt's church. Their little arms clamped around her neck told her she was needed. She didn't have to compete to be the most beautiful or most popular.

Anna clutched the Bible to her chest, while Jane's comments resurfaced in her mind. She and Jane had parted on not-so-friendly terms this afternoon.

Tears smarted behind Anna's eyes. She'd been bubbling with excitement when she told Jane about Haiti, only to have Jane accuse her of trying to run away from her problems; namely, relationships. The words had shaken her to her core. Even if she could discount Jane's psychology credentials, her insight into Ted's character had been too accurate for comfort.

But what did Jane know about ministry? Anna blinked away the tears. She pulled in a breath, forcing herself to calm down, and ruffled through the Bible pages, compelled to turn to chapter two of Genesis.

"The Lord God caused the man to fall into a deep sleep; and while he was sleeping, he took one of the man's ribs and closed up the place with flesh. Then the Lord God made a woman from the rib he had taken out of the man, and he brought her to the man. The man said, 'This is now bone of my bones and flesh of my flesh; she shall be called "woman," for she was taken out of man.'"

With an aching heart, Anna closed the Bible and set it back on the table. Time to put away that dream.

She slipped under her lavender comforter then switched off the lamp. She lay on her side, facing the window, with a view of the all-night diner across the street. Needles of rain pecked at the pane, and the sounds of the city that had taken her so long to grow used to somehow soothed her tonight.

Her eyes fluttered closed. Before sleep overcame her, she saw the handsome stranger's unshaven face. She'd seen him before—somewhere. What if she saw him again?

Anna's lips curved in a reluctant smile.

three

Daniel checked his image in the foyer mirror and straightened the knot in his tie. "All right, guy. Today's the day. Don't blow it!"

He locked his door and whistled as he strode down the red-carpeted corridor to the elevators.

The bell sounded and the doors slid open. A small silver-haired woman, clutching a poodle to her neck, stepped aside. "Good morning."

"Good morning." Daniel imagined the grin he wore looked as silly as it felt. "Cute dog."

The woman's lined face rearranged itself into a pleased smile. "Mommy loves Poochie, doesn't she?" she cooed as the elevator car sank toward the lobby. "I'm surprised she's not barking. She usually doesn't like strangers."

Daniel patted the dog's bony head, to which he got a frantic tail-wagging response. "There you go, she loves me."

Her smile broadened. "I bet everybody does, young man." With an appraising glance, she added, "Nice tie, too."

He quirked an eyebrow and tried to restrain a grin at the elderly woman's flirtation. "Thank you." With a wave, he invited her to exit the elevator ahead of him.

He held open the lobby door, watching with amusement as she set Poochie down on the sidewalk as if the tiny dog were made of glass.

Daniel waved, resumed whistling, and walked toward Third Avenue, more expectant than he'd been in a long time.

Anna. Her name was Anna.

The Sunday he ducked into church late, almost a year ago, he'd taken far more than casual notice of her. He'd called off his engagement to Paige the day before. With so much on his mind, there was no logical reason for the woman at the altar to have captured his attention. He'd stood in the shadows, smiling, listening to the tail end of her testimony as she spoke into the microphone in the sweetest voice he'd ever heard.

Since then, he'd caught glimpses of Anna, jotting down notes in church then quickly disappearing after service. He'd been praying for an opportunity to meet her, but he felt the Lord holding him back. If that wasn't enough, he noticed an austere-looking character waiting for her on the church steps after most services, too.

Daniel's brow furrowed. He couldn't picture the two belonging together. There was a sweet naiveté about Anna that just didn't fit with the gruff guy who greeted her with a curt nod and no smile.

But yesterday in the diner a small miracle had taken place. Besides learning her name, he also discovered she was free of any romantic relationship. Perfect timing!

Daniel smiled—though there had been nothing funny about his behavior. Rita Finch had met him for breakfast to discuss business. *Big business.* His attention to detail was impeccable—usually. But he'd given Rita only half an ear while straining to catch snippets of conversation from Anna's booth.

Daniel turned the corner and picked up his stride. When Anna's companion blurted, "You and Ted broke up," even Rita stopped speaking and cocked her ear to the booth behind her. He'd done his best not to laugh outright when the woman commented on Anna's baggy clothes, but her slight frame, indeed, seemed to vie for attention under too much fabric. Not having a sophisticated sense of fashion made her that much more appealing. He'd had his fill of worldly women.

Daniel shot a glance heavenward. Had the encounter in the diner been a divine appointment or a happy accident? Whatever compelled him to want to meet Anna had more to do with instinct than common sense. Her demeanor, even from afar, told me she was nothing like his social-climbing ex-fiancée, Paige.

Daniel trotted up the church steps, his gaze darting to

where the man usually stood waiting for Anna every Sunday. Hopefully, he was the infamous Ted they discussed in the diner. The one who was no longer in the picture. If not. . .

He shrugged off the realization that he'd been counting on something that might not be so. Daniel pulled open the door for a woman with a baby in one arm and a toddler gripping her other hand. Maybe someday he'd be bringing his wife and children to church. He wanted kids. Another reason things went south with Paige. The idea of ruining her body with a pregnancy repulsed her.

Daniel tucked his tie in place, strode into the sanctuary, and gazed over the milling congregation to where Anna usually sat. She hadn't arrived yet. He took a seat nearby and meditated on God's peculiar and sometimes humorous ways. The Lord must have been the one to orchestrate their meeting in the diner, allowing him to discover Anna was available. God knew his heart, and He knew he'd been drawn to Anna from the first time he'd seen her. Nothing of the kind had ever happened to him before.

For some mystifying reason, he found Anna fascinating.

The click of heels on the mosaic-tiled aisle caught his attention. Daniel looked back, and his heart gave a kick. There she was, balancing on tiptoes in search of a place to sit in the crowded chapel.

He watched as Anna picked her way carefully up the row, past two elderly women and a man with a cane, all the while whispering apologies.

When she reached the empty seat, she turned and placed her coat on the back of the pew. Their eyes met. Daniel smiled. Anna's eyes widened, and color shot into her face. She gave him a polite nod, whipped around, and dropped onto the bench.

Daniel looked at his Bible, smiling, pleased that, in this day and age, he'd made a woman blush.

❧

It's him! Anna's mind screamed as she settled into her seat.

Had he followed her? No, he'd already been sitting there. She opened her Bible and stared at it, unseeing. So this is where she knew him from. No wonder he was friendly in the diner. And to think she'd acted like a prude! The hairs on her arms prickled. *Relax. No big deal.*

Anna closed her eyes and fought to concentrate on the praise song. From now on she would shut out anything. . . *anybody*. . .that threatened to intrude on her relationship with God. She needed to prepare spiritually for the big changes about to take place in her life—and not think about the man behind her, even if he was strikingly handsome.

As she sang the chorus again, the lyrics took root in her soul. "All things work together for the good to those who love Him." She could almost touch God with her voice. The Lord's still, small voice sounded in her heart, *"To those called according to My purpose."* Not long and she would be in Haiti. Fulfilling His purpose.

The music died down, and Anna opened her eyes, watching as Pastor Meyers strode toward the pulpit. The sermons given by the lanky man with the booming voice always touched her heart as if spoken to her personally. She pulled her notebook onto her lap and readied her pen.

"How do we know when we're in the perfect will of God?" Pastor Meyers gave a crooked smile. Anna wore goose bumps. This was just what she needed to hear. She wrote *God's will* and looked up. "I can tell you from personal experience"—the pastor shook his head of sandy hair—"we know when we're *not* in His will." Anna held her breath—waiting. "We're miserable, right?" She released her breath and squirmed in her seat, resisting the urge to jump up and shout amen!

Miserable. She'd allowed herself to fall into that pit—her value reflected in Ted's eyes—for better or for worse. Mostly for worse.

Anna wrote *Out of God's will—miserable* and underlined it. So much for being labeled an oddball. She didn't need a husband or her own babies. There were enough abandoned children who needed love. She cut off the thoughts tumbling through her mind, focused her attention on the pastor, and continued taking notes.

"Today, beloved, I encourage all of you to make a commitment to be mindful of the words of Jesus, 'Love one another, as I have loved you.'"

Tears dampened Anna's eyes. She underlined *love* three times. She'd been so busy at playing at being in love with Ted, she'd hardly given real love to anybody else lately. How could she have been so deceived?

"Amen."

The collective voice of the congregation brought Anna out of her musings. She glanced at the people making their way into the aisles and then hurriedly jammed her things into her bag. Her fingers froze on the zipper. No need to rush. Ted wouldn't be waiting outside for her. A myriad of emotions assaulted her as she finished zipping her bag and picked up her purse.

"Excuse me."

Anna lifted her gaze at the sound of the silky voice with the barest hint of an accent.

There he stood—tall, dark, and handsome—like something off a movie screen.

four

He flashed her a smile and held out his hand. "Daniel Boccini." He may as well have added, *"My white horse is hitched outside."*

Anna placed her hand in his. "Hello, I'm Anna." Not Polly-Anna, but she sounded like it.

"Hello, Anna." He continued to gaze down at her with eyes so dark they almost matched the color of his coal black hair. Was he admiring her? She dismissed the notion as ridiculous and stood.

"Would you like to join me downstairs for fellowship?"

Her pulse went haywire. She draped her coat over her arm. Too dangerous, even if he was only being friendly. "That's kind of you, but—" She looked at her bag, seeing in her mind's eye the notebook inside. How about she put into practice what she had just underlined? *Love one another.* "Um, I'd like that."

"Very good."

They walked through the foyer, where Daniel held open a door leading to a wooden staircase. The aroma of coffee wafted to her nostrils. A looking-forward-to-something feeling clenched her stomach.

The next door opened into a room awash in sunlight pouring in from four arched windows. A table, set with coffee urns and bakery stood against the wall. People whom she'd never made the time to greet milled around laughing and talking.

Daniel gestured for her to go ahead of him in the food line. On a deep breath, Anna picked up two Styrofoam cups, turned with a shy smile, and handed one to him.

"Thank you." He flashed another heart-stopping smile. "Have you been in the fellowship hall before?"

She glanced away from his compelling dark eyes and

pondered the croissants. "No, I haven't." The irony hit her like a fist to her stomach. Two years of dating Ted and he had never looked at her with half as much interest. She took a gulp of air. If she was going to cry, it had better not be here or now.

An elbow caught her in the side as a woman edged between her and Daniel. "How are you, Daniel?" The model-like creature rested her hand on his arm, while Anna stood with a frozen smile on her face.

The woman appraised her with open disapproval. Anna's smile slipped. With an upward tilt of her chin, she tried to mask how ordinary she felt standing next to the stunning woman.

Daniel turned. "Brenda, this is Anna."

A whisper of jealousy fluttered across Anna's stomach. "Nice to meet you, Brenda." She had never been jealous when women talked to Ted. She forced her warmest smile to combat the base emotion.

"Nice to meet you, too," Brenda said in a crisp voice. She swung her mane of long hair over one shoulder. "Well, you look busy, Daniel, so I'll see you later." She shot Anna one last, withering glance and sauntered off.

Daniel continued to peruse the croissant tray. Was he oblivious to the flirtation or pretending to be? *Most likely the latter,* she decided, with a mental note to stop being naïve about men. Someday she might meet the *one*, and she'd have to discern such things.

Daniel turned to her suddenly, a smile in his eyes. "I hope you don't mind if I dunk."

"What?" Anna blinked as understanding dawned. "Oh, as a matter of fact, I—"

He winked. "Just kidding."

Anna smiled at his attempt to put her at ease, but he was a human magnet. With his every gesture, a delicious scent lingered—a mixture of soap and light cologne. She inched away from him, fighting her compulsion to do the opposite.

She followed him to a table with the sudden notion to take

flight. She couldn't trust herself to socialize—to say the right things—not after two years of adhering to Ted's restrictions.

Daniel set down the tray then drew back a chair for her. Anna eased into the seat and sighed inwardly. Her nerves were stretched taut as a rubber band. Maybe she was coming down with something. She opened a sugar packet, wondering how long before she spilled the hot coffee onto her lap.

Daniel sat in the chair beside hers, angling it to face her. Why hadn't he taken the seat across the table! If Jane were here, she'd be coaching. Telling her when to put a check mark in the *game player* column in her head.

Daniel tore off a piece of the croissant then switched his gaze to her. Anna looked down, unsure if she'd been gaping.

"So, Anna—what's your last name?"

"Oh, it's McCort."

"McCort." He nodded. "You don't sound like you're from New York."

"I'm not. I'm from Akron."

He tilted his head. "That's in Ohio, right?"

Anna shot him a look.

Daniel laughed. "Only kidding. I knew that."

"New Yorkers! Can't resist taking cheap shots at my home-town." She couldn't help but laugh. It broke her tension. "Thanks for buying us breakfast yesterday."

Daniel shrugged. A smooth, European shrug, she decided. "You're welcome." They could've been sitting at a table on the Via Venato in Rome. Anna stifled a sigh.

"By your reception in the diner, I guessed you didn't recognize me from church."

She was about to say *vaguely* but opted for total honesty. "No, sorry. Then again, I come and go so quickly."

"So I've noticed."

He noticed? Her heart faltered. Anna frowned as she tried to collect her scattered thoughts. Why would he notice her?

Daniel ran his hand over his five o'clock shadow. "Maybe you'd have recognized me without this. The church volunteered me to be in another play. I'm Abraham."

No doubt he wasn't familiar with not being recognized. "Really? Is that what you do? Act?"

Daniel's deep, genuine laugh took her by surprise. "Not professionally. Obviously you haven't seen me in a play, or you wouldn't have asked."

Anna looked at him over her coffee cup then redirected her gaze to a poster across the room. If she didn't know better, she'd swear he was flirting. But that made no sense, and with her past record, she couldn't afford to speculate on the inner workings of the male psyche.

"How long have you been coming to this church?" Daniel sprinkled more sugar in his coffee. She was tempted to call it *café* as he brought the cup to his lips with strong, tanned hands.

She caught herself twining a lock of hair around her finger and promptly stopped. "About a year. You?"

"Close to four years." Daniel's gaze drifted over her burning face. "You seem to be in a hurry most of the time."

Anna stared at him, mute. Ted would've flipped if he'd caught her talking to men after service. She'd become aware only lately of her personality change, altered to cater to Ted's demands. Displeasing Ted had meant being subjected to one of his jealous tirades, or worse, the silent treatment. Even now, speaking with Daniel, she feared Ted would spring out of a corner and pounce.

Daniel smiled. "Where do you work?"

She winced inwardly, suspecting he sensed her embarrassment. "At a high school called The Center, on Sixty-First Street."

Daniel snapped his fingers. "Ah, yes, I know the place. Good for you."

Anna smiled "Do you really?"

His handsome face grew pensive. "Um, yes, I know the staff helps teens who don't do well in high school. They teach them trades, right?"

Why did she suspect he was holding something back? "Yes, right. Where did you hear about The Center?"

A quick frown passed over his features. "I read about it a couple of years ago. So. . ." He sat back and undid the buttons on his jacket. She forbade her gaze to drop to his broad chest. "What's your position at the school?"

"I'm a social worker." She suddenly felt proud and humble over the progress she'd made with the teens. "Though I have been known to mop floors and take out garbage. They're short on help."

A look of concern crossed his face. "You poor woman."

Anna shook her head. "I don't mind. . .really." She hadn't meant the remark to make him think she was a martyr.

Daniel dipped his hand into the inside pocket of his jacket and retrieved a card. "I've seen their ads requesting volunteers and donations." He wrote on the blank side of the business card as he spoke. "This is my cell number." He set it in front of her. "The other side is my store," he added with a snap of his pen.

Anna picked up the card and squinted at the ornate script. *BOCCINI'S MEN'S APPAREL—ITALIAN IMPORTS.* An address on Madison Avenue. It had to be one very upscale shop. What could he possibly want of her?

Smiling, Anna waved the card around as if one day she'd have the nerve to give him a buzz.

Humor etched his dark eyes. "Perhaps you can provide me with more information on The Center, and I can help in some way."

Anna breathed a small sigh of relief, mixed with a pinch of disappointment. "Well sure, thanks." He was only being friendly. She'd love it if the Lord used her to help raise funds for The Center before she quit. She'd feel much less guilty when it came time to leave for Haiti. A list of their needs began forming in her head. She glanced at the card again. "Be careful, or I might volunteer you to coach basketball." She laughed. It felt good to joke after a humorless year with Ted.

Daniel smiled. "No problem."

Another look in his dark eyes crumbled her composure and started her knees shaking.

"Would you like to have dinner with me tonight?"

Her face grew hot. "Dinner?" This was the first time the word spelled *danger*.

His tempting mouth held a trace of a smile. "It's not a trick question."

No kidding! His type wouldn't need to trick a woman into dinner. "I—I know." Her apartment, though neat, was cluttered. Packing for Haiti would be a good idea. Dinner with Daniel might take love one another a step too far. "It's just that I have a lot to do today."

"How about tomorrow then, at seven?"

"Okay." The word blurted from her lips in spite of herself.

"Perfect." Daniel wrote down her address and phone number, while she assessed him from head to toe—from his perfectly tailored beige suit to his unscuffed, brown leather shoes. There was nothing in her wardrobe good enough for her to be seen with him. He didn't look like the fast-food type.

Daniel tucked the card and his pen back into his pocket and glanced over at her. "Are you ready?" He stood at her answering nod.

"Daniel," Brenda sang. "See you later."

Anna was hit with another pang of jealousy, quickly replaced by guilt over her aversion to the woman.

Even so, she relished the way Daniel waved at Brenda in an aloof gesture.

Some Christian I am—and only fifteen minutes after the service!

They stepped outside together, Anna's pulse racing as she watched the wind ruffle his thick, dark hair.

"Are you cold?"

Anna stared at him, taken aback by his tone. He asked seriously, as if she needed taking care of. She shrugged. "A little." She began walking backward, wondering how she'd gotten roped into dinner. *To get help for The Center,* she reassured herself.

Daniel walked toward her and touched her collar. "You need something warmer."

Warmer was not an option on her salary. She could almost hear Ted mocking. *You ought to quit that school. Zebras don't change their stripes.* He insisted the boys at The Center were beyond hope, a waste of her time. Bundling deeper into her coat, she had no regrets about refusing the big-money job Ted had offered her. Anna shook her head. "No, this is fine."

Daniel nodded, hardly looking convinced. "I turn off here. I'll see you tomorrow, at seven."

A genuine smile came to her face. "Yes, seven."

"*Ciao*, Anna McCort."

"Bye, Daniel. . ." She forgot how to pronounce his strange last name. She waved and turned, keeping her gaze fixed on the road ahead—refusing to look back.

But she couldn't restrain a smile at the sense that he was watching her walk away.

five

Anna raced up the two flights of stairs to her apartment. Of all days to get home late. But it had been crazy at The Center. Frowning, she noticed anew the crumbling plaster walls and filthy linoleum. When Daniel came to pick her up, she'd wait outside so he wouldn't see the dingy hallway.

No, she amended as she put the key in the lock. Waiting in front of the building would look pathetic. Desperate!

Anna dropped into a chair and sighed. "What a day." Things had started off wrong when Jeremy Shane limped into her office sporting a black eye. He swore his mother had nothing to do with it, but Anna strongly suspected otherwise.

The memory of Jeremy's bruised, freckled face brought a knot to her throat. If only he would fess up, the powers that be would allow her to do more to help him. She closed her eyes, sent up another silent prayer for Jeremy, and snapped on the message machine.

"Hello, Anna, I look forward to seeing you this evening." At the sound of Daniel's voice, she shot upright and clamped her teeth on her lip. "I hope you like Italian food. Seven o'clock. *Ciao.*"

A smile tugged at her mouth. She liked Italian food, but she liked Daniel's slight Italian accent even better. She replayed the tape while sorting through her mail.

Nothing but business flyers, bills, and—Anna's breath caught at the sight of an envelope with foreign stamps. She tossed aside her other mail, tore open the envelope, and skimmed over the extracted page, picking out the pertinent information. *Director of Precious Children. . .expecting her. . .looking forward to her arrival in mid-February. . .Enclosed forms. . .*

Anna grabbed a pen, smoothed the forms out on the table,

and began to fill them in.

Regret sent an ache to her heart. She should've been in Haiti last year. If only she'd never met Ted. Still, the fault was not all his. After a few months in Manhattan the knots in her stomach told her she'd made a huge mistake. She could've changed her mind at that point and gone to Haiti to join her aunt. But her stupid pride kept her here. She'd been too embarrassed to confess to friends and family that Ted didn't love her after all, though she kept praying for a miracle.

Anna frowned. Three years of college—dateless years until Ted. But her life hadn't lacked anything before Ted transferred to her college during her senior year. So why had she been so gullible?

She turned over the form to fill in the remaining blanks and expelled a weary breath. When Ted joined the campus Bible study she attended, signing the pledge vowing celibacy until marriage, she'd begun swallowing his lies. He claimed he wanted to change, to get close to God, and she had wanted to help him.

Anna wound a lock of hair around her finger. Who was she kidding? Ted wasn't the problem. She was. Even her high school prom date had been a farce. Her brother Adam asked one of his buddies to escort her. Thankfully, her parents never found out. Her mother would've blamed Anna's not having a date on all the time she spent with Aunt Mary instead of doing normal teen things. She could still see the admiration shining from her mother's face as Anna descended the stairs in her blue gown.

Tears sprang to Anna's eyes, blurring the words on the form. She grabbed a tissue, feeling foolish for crying over something that happened so long ago.

"Foolish!" She signed the forms from Precious Children and slipped them into the return envelope with a defiant nod. She'd not shed tears over a man ever again.

The phone shrilled into the quiet. Anna jumped, cleared her throat, and lifted the receiver. "Hello?"

"Hey, you."

"Oh, Jane, hi."

"I just called to find out what you're wearing for your date with the urban cowboy tonight."

Anna hesitated, glad they'd reconciled over the phone Sunday night, but afraid she'd spoken too enthusiastically about having met Daniel in church. "It's not a *date*. It's a business appointment. But I'm still debating between—"

"Can I tell you how jealous I am?" A dramatic sigh followed. "From Ted to Adonis."

"Don't even *think* of putting them in the same category. Ted was my boyfriend. Daniel's a philanthropist. I told you, he's only interested in helping The Center."

"Right."

"Honestly, now that I've had time to think on it, I'm aggravated with myself for agreeing to dinner. I had the kids' needs in mind. I didn't want to risk losing aid for the school."

"Right."

"Stop saying that. You're saying it as if you don't believe me."

"Did I say I didn't believe you?"

"Whether you do or not, I'm not going out with him again after tonight. That's definite. It's just this once—to help the school. I'm afraid your affinity for playing matchmaker has reached an all-time low."

"Right." A smile tinged Jane's voice.

"Yes, right." Anna paced. "No man can convince me to cancel another mission trip again."

"Whoa, impressive. You've only had coffee with the guy, and you're already afraid he could talk you out of Haiti?"

"I wasn't implying he could." Anna put a fist to her hip. "He couldn't." A chill traveled up her spine. Why even suggest such a ridiculous possibility?

"Did you tell Daniel you're leaving for Haiti in a couple of months?"

"Oh! Mid-February to be exact. I got the papers today."

"I see." The disappointment in Jane's voice came through clearly. "Will you tell Daniel?"

"No. Why would I?" Anna shot a glance at the clock. "It's none of his business."

"The way he looked at you in the diner, sweetie, I'd hazard a guess he'll make it his business."

Anna squelched the surge of excitement running through her and fanned her face. "You're nuts. After tonight, I'll introduce him to Joe Palmer, the principal, and they can take it from there. No need for me to get involved."

Jane's teasing chuckle echoed in her ear. "Playing it safe?"

Anna shook her head. "Are you running out of clients? Stop psychoanalyzing me. There is a spiritual side of things, you know."

"Uh-huh. Go to your closet, and I'll help you find something to wear."

After she hung up, Anna eyed the pinstriped suit Jane had helped her pick out, wondering why her friend had insisted she tell a virtual stranger about her future plans.

She shook her head. Some things were just not worth worrying about. She could handle a couple of hours with Daniel. He was charming, after all. And way too good looking for comfort, even if she were in the market for a man—which she was not.

Humming, Anna turned on the tub's faucet and poured vanilla-scented bath gel under the rush of water. She stared, mesmerized, as the amber liquid transformed into frothy white bubbles. For all Daniel's future inquiries, *if* he decided to donate funds, he could see Joe Palmer. "No problem."

Anna slipped out of her clothes, second-guessing herself on the bubble bath. Hadn't she read somewhere that men were attracted to the scent of vanilla like flies to sugar? Something like that. "Stop it, Anna!"

She stepped into the hot water and sighed. Nothing wrong with wanting to smell good.

After tonight, she'd never see Daniel again except at church.

six

At the sound of the buzzer, Anna limped to the door, one shoe on, the other in her hand. She pressed the bell to allow Daniel entrance into the hallway then glanced at the clock. Ten to seven. "The prompt type." She slipped on her other shoe and picked up her coat.

Out in the hall, she fiddled with the keys to lock the door, all the while holding her breath against the stench. Of all nights for Mrs. O'Leary's tomcats to have sprayed the hallway with megadoses of male pride.

"Anna Banana. . .it's me." Her heart stopped at the odd, singsong quality of the familiar voice. She stood frozen at her door, listening to his footfalls grow louder, closer. Ted came into view, a smile on his face. A smile that didn't reach his eyes. Icy fingers crawled up her spine. He raked his gaze over her, head to toe then back again. His smile tightened. "Where are *you* going?"

Anna straightened her shoulders. "Out."

He shook his head of curly brown hair, frizzed from the cold weather. "No, we've got to talk." His breath was on her face now, his hand gripped her shoulder. "It's important."

"I really can't." She shrugged free of his touch. "I have an appointment." How quickly he'd grown tired of his other girlfriend. Fear prickled her skin at the look in his eyes.

Ted leaned against the wall, arms crossed. She tried to keep her breaths even. Any show of emotion, and he'd perceive it as an inroad.

The bell sounded from behind her door.

"Ted, I have to go." Anna brushed past him, picturing Daniel waiting downstairs, getting no response to the bell. What if she got Daniel, an innocent bystander, involved in a fistfight? She had never put a match to Ted's short fuse before.

"Where are you going?" Ted growled close to her ear, sending chills down her neck.

Anna reached the first landing, stopped, and turned to face him. "I have a business meeting. We'll talk tomorrow, okay?"

His eyes narrowed. He seemed to sense her growing panic like a hound did fresh blood. The color drained from his face. "What? I make one mistake, and you're already gallivanting?"

"Gallivanting? I told you, this is business." Anna turned, taking the stairs slowly on wobbly legs.

"What time tomorrow?" Ted's tone, more insistent, was meant to disturb her neighbors. Meant to force her into agreeing on a time to avoid a scene.

Her textbook knowledge on how to diffuse a violent situation flew out of her head. *Remain calm*, she recalled, trembling harder.

seven

Anna spotted Daniel behind the locked glass door. *Oh Lord, please help me reach him!*

She glanced over her shoulder. Ted hung back, midway on the staircase, out of Daniel's view.

"Better find a way to get out of this, Anna." Ted's voice carried a clear threat. What had happened to him?

Anna walked slowly toward Daniel, praying away the threat of Ted's menacing presence behind her. The thudding of Ted's footfalls on the stairs filled her ears, closing in on her. Anna stopped.

Daniel's eyes flashed to a spot above her, his smile disappeared. He jiggled the knob, causing the glass panes to rattle in their frames.

"You can still get out of this." Ted's words grated between clenched teeth. The fake smile in his voice chilled her.

Fear kept her feet planted to the floor. *Move!* She sucked in a breath and walked forward. The walls seemed to grow narrower, squeezing the breath out of her.

Daniel rattled the knob again.

Anna grasped the handle and pulled hard. Swinging open the door, her shoe heel dug into Ted's sneaker. Ted jabbed his finger hard into her back. Daniel's scent rolled over her. She exhaled a jagged sigh. *Oh, thank You, Lord, I'm safe, for now.*

Daniel clamped his hands to her upper arms, looking down into her face. "Are you all right?"

"Yes, fine." Anna licked her parched lips. "Fine."

"I'm Ted." His hot breath swept across her neck. "Anna's fiancé." He sounded as if he owned her. The pressure of Ted's body against her back made her stomach pitch.

Anna opened her mouth to clear up the misconception, but

Daniel took her by the arm and eased her behind him.

"That isn't true." Daniel's silky voice held a razor-sharp edge.

"Huh?" Ted snorted a mocking chuckle. "Tell him, Anna."

She peered over Daniel's shoulder, keeping her gaze steady on Ted's face and balled her shaky hands into fists. "You're not my fiancé. . .anymore." Her voice cracked. She drew a breath, assessing the danger anew. Daniel and Ted both stood a little over six feet in height. Daniel was broader. Maybe Ted would back down.

Ted's eyes bulged in silent challenge. Sandwiched between the mailboxes and Daniel's back, she felt Daniel's muscles tighten under his suit jacket.

She had once loved Ted—when she believed he was sincere about his faith—and thought he loved her, too. But now, with his face contorted in a jealous rage, pity replaced any love she'd once felt for him. Pity—and fear.

Ted opened his mouth then snapped it shut. He jammed one hand in the pocket of his denim jacket, the other on the door leading to the street. "This ain't over." He brushed past them. "Tomorrow, Anna."

The door swung back. Anna sagged against the wall, staring at the floor.

Daniel turned. "Are you all right?"

Anna lifted her gaze, gripping Daniel's forearm to keep steady. "I'm so sorry."

"You're sorry?" Daniel shook his head. "Sorry for what?"

"Ted. . .he. . ." She fought for deeper breaths. "I didn't mean for you to get involved in this."

Daniel shot a glance at the door facing the street. He plowed his fingers through his hair and turned to her again. "Do you want to kiss and make up with that guy?"

"No!" She gazed into his eyes. "No, it's over."

"All right." Daniel nodded. "You have nothing to worry about. If he bothers you again I'll—"

"Oh, he won't." Anna shook her head. Whatever she saw smoldering in Daniel's dark eyes prompted her to defend Ted.

"I'm sure he won't come back." A shiver of uncertainty crept up her spine. What if he came back to kill her? Ted had been like a stranger in a dark alley tonight. In her line of work, she knew people were murdered for lesser motives.

Daniel nodded. "We'll discuss Ted later."

A tremulous smile inched across her lips. "Yes, fine." As her breathing slowed, she drank in the sight of Daniel. His thick black hair, brushed away from his face, barely grazed the collar of his white shirt. He looked strong and courageous. He'd defended her though they were practically strangers. "Thank you for helping—"

"No need." Daniel took charge of the coat hanging over her arm. "It's chilly, better put this on."

Anna slipped into it and tied the belt, reliving the look on Ted's face. A deep-down chill sent a shiver through her. She fastened her gaze on Daniel and felt herself relaxing.

Daniel fingered the lapel of his pinstriped suit. "We match."

His good-natured tone reassured her he didn't hold her responsible for the ugly scene. "Yes, we do."

They stepped outside, her legs still trembling as she watched Daniel walk up to a double-parked limo. Anna halted at the curb.

Holding open the car door, Daniel coaxed her with a wave. "Please."

Anna took hesitant steps to the car. She leaned in, instantly welcomed by the scent of leather, and glanced over her shoulder. "Daniel, a limo?"

He slid in beside her, closed the door, and spoke Italian to the driver whom Anna couldn't see through the smoky glass divider. A woman responded in Italian as the car merged into traffic.

Anna's gaze swept the car's interior, which muted the sounds of Manhattan traffic. "This is my first time in a limo."

"Is that right?" Daniel's dark brows pulled together, same as when she had told him she hauled garbage at The Center. "My grandpa started the limo business when he came here from Naples. Now it's my uncle's."

"How nice."

Daniel leaned forward to the adjacent bench seat. "I have something for you." He picked up a bouquet wrapped in paper and offered it to her.

Anna stared long and hard at the gift in her hands. "For me?" While out on business? What does he do for a date? As she removed the paper, each tear released a sweeter fragrance into the car. "Oh, Daniel, how beautiful!" She cleared her throat. "White roses." Tears rushed to her eyes. She inhaled their scent, afraid to look at him. "Thank you."

"My pleasure."

Anna touched the petals of the lavish gift then buried her nose in their cotton-soft texture. Flowers shouldn't make her feel so sad—or scared. She sensed she was heading for trouble. She couldn't wait to run from all this—leave her messy life and the memories behind. Haiti was only a heartbeat away. The thought eased the tension in her stomach.

Daniel drew the bouquet away from her face. She gave him a sideways glance. Empathy flashed in his eyes.

"Are you sure you're all right?" He brushed back her hair. "Are you upset about the awful incident back there?"

"No, I'm fine." What must he think of her? Anna cradled the bouquet closer to her chest.

"Who could blame you if. . ." Daniel drew an audible breath. "I'm sure any woman would be intimidated by—"

"Ted?" Anna shook her head. "I'm okay now."

Daniel sighed, looking unconvinced. He tugged at his tie and nodded, as if he'd settled something in his mind. "Time to change the subject." He rested against the seat and unbuttoned his jacket. "Now, I know you're from Akron, and you're a social worker. Tell me about your family."

Anna took a deep breath, in an attempt to cover her strange reaction to the flowers. "I have a brother and a sister, both older." She clutched the stems of the bouquet tighter. "My brother Adam is single and lives in a tacky bachelor's pad with a—"

"Wait." Daniel held up his hand. "Let me guess. A faux

leopard-skin rug in front of the fireplace?"

Laughing, Anna shook her head. "Not quite that bad, but close enough." This didn't feel like a business meeting. She cleared her throat and sat up straighter. "My sister Lynn is married and has two adorable sons." A picture of their faces flitted through her mind. She smiled. "They're great kids."

"Ah!" Daniel nodded. "You sound like you love children."

"Yes, I do." The words came out too wistfully. "I can't wait to have. . ." *A baby*. But her heartstrings were all tangled up. Ted had been the only possibility in her life, and tonight she knew for certain it was over.

"I love children, too. I hope to have a house full of them some day."

Though his tone was serious, Anna looked at him to see if he was joking. He met her gaze and held it. She forced herself to look away, trying not to ponder the exchange.

"And your parents?"

A sudden pang of longing hit. If her mom could see her, riding in a limo with a man who looked like a movie star, she'd no doubt mistake the grand scenario for a real date. *Poor Mom*. But maybe all mothers thought their daughters worthy of knights in shining armor.

"Mom and Dad live in Akron, in the same little house where I grew up. Dad's a postal carrier, and Mom's in marketing."

"I imagine you miss them." He moved forward and snapped open a wooden door panel. "Would you like something to drink?"

Anna stared into the mini refrigerator. *A fridge in a car?* "Water would be great."

Daniel grabbed two bottles, twisted off the cap on one, and handed it to her. "How did you wind up living in Manhattan, Anna?"

"My fiancé. . .my ex-fiancé is from New York. Ted. The one you just. . .bumped into." She squeezed the bottle so hard it made a popping sound. "We met in college and I. . .and we—"

"What college did you attend?"

She wanted to kiss him for changing the subject. Oh no, not actually *kiss* him. . . "I—I went to University of Tennessee."

"I regret not attending an—"

The car swerved left, depositing her against Daniel's solid arm. An itchy sweat broke out on her forehead.

"As I was saying"—Daniel smiled as though he didn't notice their nearness—"I regret not attending an out of state university. I bet I missed a lot not living on campus."

"You definitely did!" Sheer nerves made her blurt the stupid remark.

Daniel laughed. "At least you're honest." He scanned her face, which she imagined was a guilty shade of scarlet. "You're a breath of fresh air, Anna."

She glanced away with an urge to run. To hide. To go home, crawl under her comforter, and never come out. "Where did you go to college?"

"NYU."

"Impressive." Jane would die when she told her. Jane blatantly admitted she'd date a troll as long as he was brainy. Anna restrained a smile at the errant thought. "What was your major?"

"Business, eventually. But first I spent time dabbling in courses that wouldn't have gotten me far running my family's businesses." He took a drink of water while she admired his profile.

She gripped the flower stems tighter yet. "What kinds of courses?"

"Philosophy, archaeology, that sort of thing. Thinking back," he said, "my parents were furious."

"No kidding?" Anna frowned. "Why would they be?"

"I guess I was too eccentric for their taste." He shrugged. "I can't blame them. I have no siblings. They're depending on me to run their businesses."

Anna summoned a cheery voice. "Well, that's nice." Was he living out his parents' dreams instead of his own? She gazed out the side window with a renewed appreciation for her mom and dad. At least they'd encouraged her to follow her aspirations career-wise, if not in Aunt Mary's footsteps.

Daniel nudged her. "How old are you?"

Anna blinked at the unexpected question. "I'll be twenty-five soon."

"When's your birthday?"

Curious type, she mused, flattered by his interest. "November nineteenth."

"Hmm, I'll have to remember that." Daniel stared off for a moment. "I'll be twenty-nine January first."

"New Year's Day." Nearly thirty and he hadn't been taken? Was there something wrong with him, or was he biding his time, waiting for the right woman? Another thought sprang to life, replacing her wonder with cynical reality. He was probably divorced. "Have you ever been married?" Anna clamped her teeth on her lower lip. So much for her metamorphosis tonight—from mousy to mouthy.

Daniel faced her and paused. It would serve her right if he said it was none of her business. "Almost."

Almost married? She had to bite her tongue to refrain from digging for more. Had he broken the engagement? Or had his fiancée? And why? Maybe Brenda had been the woman he'd almost married. Her stomach cinched.

The glass divider slid open, and the driver rattled off something in Italian. The window snapped shut just as quickly.

Smiling, Daniel shook his head. "Sorry about the Italian. The driver, Nicole, is my cousin. She's been in the States for only six months and doesn't speak English very well."

"What did she say?" Anna winced. "Sorry for asking."

"No need to be sorry." Daniel brushed at his perfectly tailored jacket. "Just Nicole being Nicole. She's a born matchmaker."

"Matchmaker?" Anna mouthed the word. A wild urge to fling open the car door and flee hit her again.

eight

Daniel gazed out the window. "A few blocks and we're there."

Anna looked past him out the side window. "Where are we?"

"Little Italy."

Anna peered at the row of eateries and stores, shoved her concerns aside, and smiled. "I've been dying to come here."

His brows shot up. "You've lived in Manhattan a year, and you've never been to Little Italy?"

"Well, Ted wasn't one for going out much." *Keep babbling, Anna!* He knew nearly as much about her pathetic personal life as Jane did.

"What do you know?" Daniel crossed his arms and gave a satisfied nod. "I get to introduce you to two new things tonight—a limo and Little Italy. I hoped to impress you."

And the flowers. Another first. She possessed enough of her faculties to know better than to mention that embarrassing fact.

The tires crackled over the pebbly street, and the car rolled to a stop. "Here we are." Daniel pointed.

Anna read the gold script across the restaurant window and gasped. "Boccini's Ristorante?"

"I forgot to mention my Uncle George owns it."

Born with a silver spoon! "I guess he's not the same uncle who owns the limo business?" She wanted to grab back the words. The sarcasm wasn't deliberate.

"No. All the men in our family choose their own enterprises."

Anna managed a smile. She had no right making assumptions about wealthy people. She ran a quick gaze over Daniel. He seemed kind. Gentle, even.

She sat up straighter. What did she know! It would be a long time—if ever—before she'd trust her instincts about men.

And this European charmer was not a romantic possibility. She must be suffering posttraumatic Ted syndrome.

The car door swung open. Anna looked up at Daniel's cousin. "*Ciao*," she said, leaning farther into the car. Raven locks fell forward, framing her cherubic face.

"Hello." Anna stepped outside and noticed Nicole give Daniel a wink.

Her pulse sped. What if Nicole *was* playing at matchmaker? But, no. Daniel had made it clear he was only interested in helping The Center.

"Anna, this is my cousin, Nicole."

Anna offered her hand, but Nicole clutched her by the shoulders and kissed her on either cheek. "Beautiful," Nicole said. "You have a beautiful time." She hopped into the front seat, closed the door, and honked a good-bye.

Daniel opened the restaurant door, turned, and leaned down. With his handsome face so close to hers in the tiny foyer, she called on God for help. She clung to the notion that her heart-thudding response to his nearness was the result of dating inexperience. Nothing more.

"I think I should warn you," he whispered, "my family is a little exuberant."

Anna gave a casual wave. "They're Italian, right?"

Daniel winked. "Ah, then you understand."

They stepped inside the white-tiled room. Anna unbuttoned her coat, inhaling the delicious food smells, when a group of strangers converged on her.

"This is Anna, everybody." Daniel stepped back and leaned against the wall.

"I'm Daniel's uncle." The stout man pinched her cheek. "*Bella!* One look at you and I can tell you're too good for this guy." He motioned to Daniel with his chin.

Anna was about to protest, but another man, tall and somber, removed her coat before she had a chance to thank him. Someone else gave a short bow and said, "Follow me, I'll give you the best seats in the house."

"What did I tell you?" Daniel whispered as they made their way to the table. He thanked his uncle, pulled out a chair for her at the table for four, and then settled into the seat opposite hers. "You have the most beautiful eyes, Anna."

She held her breath, waiting for him to punctuate with something negative as Ted would've done, but a kind smile followed.

"Thank you." Anna dropped her gaze to the white table-cloth. No man had ever spoken to her this way or treated her as if she were royalty. She half expected someone to tap her on the shoulder and say, "Sorry, there's been some mistake."

☙

Daniel watched the candlelight play on Anna's sweet face, illuminating her turquoise eyes—their centers splashed with gold. In his heart, he had always believed in love at first sight. Even when Anna was serious, her lips turned up at their corners. He pushed away his impulse to kiss those lips and instead rose from his seat. "You're sitting too far from me."

Anna's gaze followed him as he came around the table and sat in the chair beside hers. She cleared her throat. "Oh, fine, I. . ."

"Besides." Daniel picked up the menu. "A blondie from Akron will never understand this menu."

Anna's brows furrowed. "You're probably right. Jane says we're all-American generics. That some day we'll marry two men from Connecticut named Kyle." She laughed.

Daniel shook his head. "Impossible, I saw you first."

Anna's eyes flashed like big blinking caution lights. He wanted to slap his hand to his forehead. He hated his penchant for impatience. He had bungled things enough in the fellowship hall. Eventually, he'd have to confess.

His uncle George set an antipasto platter atop the table.

Anna smiled her approval and put her hand to her cheek. He noted the only jewelry on her graceful fingers was a silver ring in the shape of a cross. Her unfussy appearance only enhanced her natural beauty.

Daniel rubbed his hands together. "Let's pray."

Anna placed her hand in his. He clasped his fingers around her smooth, cool hand and closed his eyes.

Aloud, he thanked God for the food, and inwardly he thanked Him for the opportunity to be with Anna. He would follow this road, hoping it led him closer to his heart's desire. His history with the likes of Paige was over. He was past ready to share all his God-given blessings with a family.

As each course was served, he pretended not to notice Anna devour every morsel from her plate—in the most ladylike way. He gave her a sideways glance. "Enjoy everything?"

"Too much, I'm afraid." She sighed. "You must think I haven't eaten in weeks."

"Weeks?" Daniel laughed. "Months!"

Anna cringed. "I've made a glutton of myself."

"No, no. I love that you love to eat." The memory of Paige and her salad diet flashed through his mind. Daniel's smile disappeared. "I don't like dating rabbits." *Oh no!* He'd done it again!

Anna stiffened enough to make his heart sink. She reached down and picked up her purse. "I have information on The Center." She retrieved an envelope from her bag and set it on the table with finality.

Daniel stared at the envelope between them. The Center. The only reason she agreed to see him. "Yes, thank you." The Center. The school his board had turned down for a grant a couple of years ago. A small point he neglected to tell her at church. His guilt had driven him to see the principal this morning and drop off a hefty donation from his personal funds. Still, the whole thing smacked of deviousness.

The squeaking dessert-cart wheels brought him out of his morose musings.

"What would the young lady like?" His uncle moved the cart closer to Anna.

Anna crossed her arm over her stomach. "No, thank you. I just couldn't." She darted a glance at Daniel. "I really have to go anyway."

George wagged his finger. "Nobody leaves Boccini's without dessert."

"Uncle, she must leave." Another push in the wrong direction and he'd never see her again. "Why don't you wrap something for Anna to take home?"

George groaned. "Ah, too bad." He looked at Anna and shrugged. "So, what do you have?"

Pointing to the cheesecake, Anna licked her lips. "Looks great."

"The best!" George gave a short bow. "I pack for you."

Daniel pulled out his cell phone and signaled for Nicole to bring the car around. On a scale of one to ten, he rated the evening a cautiously optimistic seven.

He deducted a point on their way out the door when his uncle gave them a thumbs-up and a broad wink.

Halfway into the ride home, Daniel broke the silence. "Did you have a nice evening?"

Anna nodded. "Yes. Absolutely."

"Great." Daniel clenched his jaw in an effort to keep from asking her out again. "That's what I was hoping."

"A limousine. Flowers." Smoothing her hand over the bag holding the dessert, she added, "The best meal I've eaten in my entire life." She smiled. "Thanks for everything, Daniel."

For him, the conclusion of a date. For Anna, the conclusion. Period. Daniel sighed. Getting shot down had never stopped him from getting up before. A plan was already forming in his head. Ted's cruel behavior had told him he'd have to work for Anna's trust, and he'd have to protect her. He had never been so close to hitting a man in all his life.

Daniel stared at his clenched fists and tried to steady his breathing. "What kind of work does Ted do?"

Anna released the lock of hair coiled around her finger. "He's an insurance investigator."

A doomsday feeling brought him up straight. "You can't go back to your apartment tonight."

Anna's eyes widened; then she laughed. "Believe me, you

saw Ted at his worst." She began to gather her belongings. "He won't come back." She lifted her chin a notch. "Even if he does, I'm not afraid of him."

Daniel scrubbed his hand across his jaw, reserving comment. He hadn't the heart to remind her of her earlier response to Ted's bullying.

The car stopped in front of her red brick tenement. "Daniel, thanks—"

"I'll walk you up."

Nicole opened the car door.

"That won't be necessary." Anna stepped out of the car. "Good night, Nicole."

He followed Anna, turned, and asked Nicole to wait. With the possibility of Ted lurking in the shadows, he shoved aside all sense of propriety and pride. "Anna, allow me to walk you to your door."

She struggled with the items in her hands while trying to insert the key into the lock of the foyer door. "Let me hold those for you."

Anna handed him the paper bag and the flowers. "Thanks, but I've been living here alone for a year." She pushed open the door. "I'll be fine." She plucked the flowers and paper bag from his hands.

Daniel followed her to the edge of the staircase. "I'll stand here until you're inside your apartment and you ring the bell."

"All right." She tilted her head. "If it'll make you feel better." She giggled then started up the stairs. "Thanks for everything."

"You're welcome." He watched her with growing agitation until she reached the top of the staircase. "Does Ted have a key to your apartment?"

Anna turned and looked down. "Don't worry. He doesn't. I'll buzz when I get inside."

"Yes, good. I'll see you then." He listened to her diminishing footsteps with dread. He didn't hear her door open or close, but the buzzer sounded. Pacing, he waited another minute before exiting the building.

In the car, it struck him that he should've asked more questions about Ted, even if Anna was put off by it. He stared out at the blur of passing lights. *Lord, please keep Anna safe. I trust you to protect her.*

An unwelcome memory of the daggers in Ted's eyes hit him. Suppose Ted had been waiting in Anna's apartment? Rang the bell himself? Daniel shook his head. Anna seemed certain he wouldn't be back. Or was she covering for Ted?

Nicole slid open the divider, shaking him out of his morbid revelry. "Will you see Anna again?"

"Tomorrow, Nicole. Tomorrow."

nine

Anna lifted the stack of folders from her desk and carried them to the file cabinet. She glanced at the clock and sighed. Most of the morning had dwindled while she'd done nothing but clear away clutter. So much for being a neat freak. She was always tidying up for her disorganized coworkers.

A phone memo floated to the floor. Anna picked it up. *From the desk of Joe Palmer. URGENT.*

"No date on this?" Anna grabbed the phone and punched in Joe's extension, praying none of the students had met with trouble. While she waited for Joe to pick up, her thoughts drifted to Daniel. She closed her eyes. She hadn't meant to be abrupt last night, but the more kindness and consideration Daniel showed her, the more she contrasted his behavior with Ted's, the more restless she'd become. Why had Daniel asked her to dinner? He could've come to the school to discuss the grant.

Anna frowned. Why was she wasting time thinking about it? There was no sense mulling over Daniel's words. *I don't like dating rabbits.* Dating? She was doing it again. Wasting valuable time analyzing a man she'd never see outside of church.

Anna shook her head, set down the phone, and sighed. This morning she had dropped the forms to Precious Children in the mailbox. Her aunt was depending on her. There was no turning back now. The thought brought a sense of freedom— and fear, all at once.

The phone rang, giving her a start. Since Ted's visit last night, she jumped at the slightest provocation. Her paranoia had her suspecting the letter from Haiti in her apartment had been moved from one spot to another. "Crazy." She picked up the phone. "Anna McCort."

"Good, you haven't left for lunch yet. I'm on my way up."

Anna bolted from her chair and glanced in the wall mirror. "Daniel? On your way up? Up *here*?" She searched her purse for lipstick, dabbed pink on her lips, and slipped the tube into her pocket.

"Are you surprised?" His warm laughter traveled to her ear, bringing a reticent smile to her face.

"Yes, very." Her smile turned into a grimace. There was nothing funny about seeing Daniel Boccini again. This had to stop. She would make that clear the second he walked through the door.

"Anna."

She pivoted. Daniel stood in the doorway to her office, cell phone in hand. He looked dashing in a gray silk shirt and black trousers. His dark eyes held her still while her head swirled. She swallowed the words she had prepared to fire off at him. "Hi." She stared at the phone in her hand then set it down.

"Hello to you." Daniel crossed the room and placed a blue vinyl case atop her desk. "You look like a woman who could use a good, hot lunch today." He unzipped the case, filling the room with a delicious, saucy-smelling aroma.

"You brought me lunch?" Anna peered into the case, her pulse racing. "I usually skip lunch, but. . ." She pressed her hand to her stomach.

"What?"

Anna sat. "What?"

Daniel peeled back the foil and paper from the sandwiches. "You were saying you usually skip lunch." He cocked his head.

Anna licked her lips, longing for just a taste of the sandwich on seeded Italian bread. "I guess I'm hungry today."

Daniel leaned across the desk and patted her cheek. "Good."

He produced two cloth napkins, real silver silverware, two stemmed glasses, and a bottle of sparkling cider. "This," he said, taking the chair in front of her desk, "is an eggplant hero."

"Oh, my." Anna tucked her hair behind her ears, grinning. Struck by his uncanny sense of timing, she lifted her gaze to him. "How did you know I take lunch at eleven thirty?"

He winked. "I phoned and inquired."

"To whom did you speak?" Anna glanced at the hero that made her stomach growl with longing. She switched her gaze to Daniel and crashed head-on with his dark eyes. After lunch, she would tell him she couldn't make any more appointments with him. She would tell him to see Joe about anything grant related. Definitely. She tugged at her bulky sweater. "They're extremely security conscious around here. Nobody but staff is allowed into the building, usually."

"Don't worry." Daniel gestured with his nonchalant shrug. "I have connections."

"I bet you do." Anna lifted the hero to her lips.

"Wait. We didn't pray."

She promptly released the sandwich. "You're right." Since when had she forgotten to thank God for her food? The tall, dark, handsome thing shouldn't be affecting her. Any normal woman would still be grieving her breakup. Of course "normal" had never been her strong suit.

Anna clasped her hands and closed her eyes. She'd bring everything to a screeching halt after lunch.

❧

Daniel said a prayer then eyed Anna discreetly, restraining a smile as they ate. Her first bite was a nibble, and the ones that followed were heartier and accompanied by hums of pleasure. "Tell me, do you like the sandwich?"

Nodding, she swallowed. "Delicious."

"I made them myself."

Anna blinked. A shy grin followed. "No, you didn't. You're putting me on."

"Yes, I did. Made from scratch in my kitchen."

Her smile disappeared. "So you can cook, too?"

What did she mean by that? Daniel leaned back against the chair. "You sound upset."

Frowning, she shook her head. "We need to talk, Daniel."

Uh-oh. Bad news was about to hit him like an arrow between the eyes. He raked his mind for a change of topic. "I have a surprise dessert for you." He reached into the container.

"No, no." Anna sat very straight in her chair. "You'll get me fat."

He pulled back his hand. "If we're going to be friends, you'll have to learn to love to eat." That should please her. Friendship. No pressure. But she cast a glance downward, spending too much time staring at the desk. He sensed she was gathering her strength for a good-bye speech.

"So, Anna." He must find a way to further divert her attention. "Do you like working here?"

Daniel surveyed the dreary surroundings. One sooty window overlooked the basketball court. The dark wood-paneled walls matched the scarred desk and chairs. A noisy radiator clanged out heat.

"I believe this is where God called me." She began cleaning up the desk. "For now."

"Interesting." Daniel capped the cider. "My life just sort of happened. I always knew my parents' businesses would be mine. It wasn't as if I asked God—or anything." He sighed, His own words somehow made him feel spiritually inadequate.

"Don't worry." Anna's empathetic smile told him she'd read him like an open book. "You're called by God in a different way. For instance, helping The Center." Her smile broadened. "All the needs out there, yet you chose this one."

Daniel's breath caught. He'd been deceptive for using the school as the sole excuse to see Anna. This was the first time in his life he had to contrive a story to convince a woman to go out with him. Now he had an uneasy conscience to go with his bruised ego.

Anna's brows arched. "As I was about to say, Daniel"—she tugged at her sweater—"we won't be able to—"

A quick rap at the door grabbed Anna's attention. Daniel released a long breath. Just in time!

&

Joe Palmer poked his head around the door. "Hey, I don't want to interrupt."

Since when? Anna mused. Joe barged into her office whenever he pleased and usually with fifteen demands at the same time.

Joe stepped into the room, nodded towards Daniel. "Mr. Boccini."

Mr. Boccini? Anna looked from Joe to Daniel. Apparently, they'd met. But when?

The men shook hands. "I can come back later." Joe sent a sly wink her way.

"No, please." Daniel looked at Joe. "I'm late for a meeting." He reached into the case. "But first, the surprise I promised you, Anna." He handed her something cold and rectangular, wrapped in foil. "After all, you did finish your lunch."

Smiling, Joe glanced at his watch. "I think I will come back later."

Anna wanted to snag Joe by the shirt, but the door snapped behind him, leaving her alone again to deal with the handsome Italian.

To fill the awkward silence, she removed the foil wrapper. "A Hershey bar? My favorite. And it's cold."

Daniel's dark gaze latched onto hers. "One day I'll dazzle you with one of my special desserts." He took another step closer to her on his way out of the office. "I can be very dangerous in the kitchen."

In the kitchen? Anywhere! Dizzied by his delicious scent, the warmth of the room, and his lips nearly touching hers, Anna gulped and stared at the candy bar. "Thank you for. . ."

Daniel leaned closer, and something brushed her cheek. "You're welcome, Anna."

Had he kissed her? She ought to move. She wasn't trapped—except by her own desire to savor his nearness. She forced her arms to remain at her sides lest she reach up and hug him.

Daniel cleared his throat. "I'd better go."

Anna nodded, unable to meet his gaze, then mumbled something even she didn't understand.

As soon as the door closed behind him, she collapsed in her

chair. Had he kissed her? Or was it his chin that had brushed her cheek? She shook her head. What did she think she was doing? "I've got to get back to work."

She tore the paper off the chocolate bar, snapped off two large pieces, and then stuffed them into her mouth. She stared out the window in stunned silence. She'd have to do everything within her power to avoid seeing Daniel again. She'd vowed to forgo romantic notions for a much greater cause.

"I'm not a spiritual weakling," she mumbled around a mouthful of chocolate. What just happened? It would be absurd to think she was in love with a man she'd met three times. God's servants didn't run around like the Three Stooges, tripping all over themselves, emotions in high gear.

She was a woman of God. The horrible mistake—missing God's guidance to be with Ted—had been a wake-up call. Now she'd stay on high alert. Wanting Daniel to kiss her had been a crazy, momentary lapse in judgment. Nothing to worry about.

Anna reached for more chocolate, discovering an empty wrapper. She lifted papers, searching as if a thief had snatched it when she wasn't looking. She crossed her arm over her too-full stomach and jumped at the rap on the door.

Joe swept into the room. "You've got chocolate all over your mouth, young lady." Laughing, he ran his splayed fingers over his baldhead.

"Hi, Joe." With as much finesse as she could muster, Anna dabbed a tissue to her lips. But she was fraying at the seams. She couldn't shake the lingering guilt of wanting Daniel to kiss her.

"Listen up." Joe dropped into a chair.

"Something wrong with one of the kids? I came across your phone message." She itched to ask Joe how he knew Daniel, but her boss was the tight-lipped sort and she'd been unprofessional enough for one day.

"Nothing wrong with the kids." He shrugged. "Forget my message. Another near crisis that's been resolved." Joe cleared his throat. "I'm here to talk about Daniel."

"Da—Da—Daniel?" Great! Now she was stuttering. Her face flamed with embarrassment. The mere mention of his name turned her into a babbling idiot. *Please, Lord, don't let Joe notice.*

Joe slid to the edge of his chair, eyes narrowed. "I guess you know he's a benefactor," he said, his tone low and solemn.

"Of this school?" Anna massaged her temples. Was she dreaming this confusion? "Since when?"

"Since yesterday." Joe smiled. "What a way to start Monday morning. Daniel came by with a big, fat check. You must've made some impression on him."

"Me?" Anna pointed at her guilty self. "I'd like to take the credit, Joe, but we spoke briefly after Sunday service and not much about The Center." She'd been too busy getting lost in his dark eyes.

Anna swept her gaze over her boss. He fidgeted, looking more agitated by the second, and cleared his throat twice. "Whatever you did, you made a great impression." Joe stood. "That's why I'm here." He rubbed his hairless dome again. "I want you to spend a little time with Daniel and—"

"What? Why?" Anna bolted from her chair. "No, I can't!"

Joe waved in a calm-down gesture. "Anna, I don't know what you've got against the guy, but I do know how much you care about the kids here."

"Of course I do." Why else would she put in extra hours without pay? Working in another sector, she could've earned more money with much less hassle.

"And Mr. Boccini. . .Daniel is sincere about helping."

Anna crossed her arms over her jittery midsection. "What does any of this have to do with me?"

"First off, he's accountable to a board who decides where money goes, how much, and to whom. You get the picture."

Anna sat without taking her gaze off Joe's face. She'd listen just to be polite.

"I don't have to tell you how desperate we are for funds." Joe sighed. "The paperwork and grant proposals I can handle. But let's face it, I'm not exactly Mr. Personality."

Anna would've liked to disagree with him. She averted her gaze. "What are you suggesting, Joe?"

"What I'm asking should take all of two, maybe three meetings with Daniel. I'll give you the papers. You just present them to him, show him around the facilities, answer questions he might have."

"Are you saying Daniel won't give the school more money unless I go out with him?" Anna's stomach tightened. Somewhere in her shameful heart, she hoped Daniel had manipulated circumstances to see her again.

"No way!" Joe's forceful response made her shrink back to her rightful size. "But I'm certain he'd prefer your company to mine, if that's what you're implying."

"I didn't mean. . ." Anna took a steadying breath. Hadn't Daniel kissed her? Maybe she had leaned forward, his lips touched her cheek and. . .

She was losing her mind! Moments ago, Daniel had referred to her as a friend. She was panicking over nothing—probably.

"Anna? Will you do this for us?"

Guilt washed over her. Soon she'd be leaving The Center. This would be her last good deed. She'd always dreamed of doing something for the greater good. This was her chance.

Anna released the tangle of hair cutting off the circulation in her finger. "Okay. What do you want me to do?"

ten

Anna flipped the steaks in the pan. How good to be having company tonight—a reason to cook. For three days she'd been drowning her disappointment in Chang's wonton soup, secretly hoping Daniel would call.

Anna stirred the potatoes bobbing to the top of the bubbling water. Maybe Daniel would never call. Joe Palmer said Daniel had given The Center a huge donation. If that was the extent of Daniel's generosity, she should be grateful.

She clamped the lid on the pot and glanced at the calendar on her refrigerator. Before bedtime, she would draw a line through October 30, a day closer to leaving for Haiti. God had worked it out for the best. If true love ever did come her way, maybe the Lord would perform a miracle—a sign—a flash from the heavens and His voice saying, *"This is the man whose rib you've been fashioned from, Anna."*

The shrill of the bell interrupted her wild daydream. "She's on time!" Anna set down the spoon, reached over, and pressed the bell to open the door downstairs. When would the landlord install an intercom system? Probably after she moved.

She lowered the flame under the steaks, went to the front door, and opened it. Standing partway in the hall, Anna smiled as she listened to Jane pounding up the steps.

Her panting friend came into view and pulled a scowl. "Those stairs will be the death of me." She brushed past Anna into the kitchen.

"I knew you'd say that." Anna closed and locked the door. "I can't believe you're on time."

"Gee, thanks." Wearing a grin, Jane dangled a bakery box in front of her eyes. "Dessert. Because I can always use the extra padding on my thighs."

Laughing, Anna gave the box a shake. "What's in it?" She set the box on the kitchen counter and returned to the stove.

"Not telling." Jane sat. "It's a surprise."

The words brought a reminder of Daniel and his lunchtime surprise. Had Daniel kissed her? Or not? Anna glanced over her shoulder at Jane, afraid her friend could read her thoughts. She stirred the frying onions, making an effort to concentrate on cooking. "The steaks are almost done."

Jane stood. "You didn't have to go to so much trouble. And look at how pretty you set the table."

"No trouble at all." Anna brought the pot of potatoes to the sink. Jane had done her a favor, dropping her own plans to occupy a do-nothing Thursday evening. "It feels great to be cooking for someone again."

"I wouldn't know." Jane stopped circling the kitchen. "You've turned this dinky, little apartment into a country cottage. You almost make *me* want to be the next Martha Stewart—not!" Laughing, she meandered to the stove. "Can I help?"

With her hands busy mashing the potatoes, Anna jutted her chin toward the cabinet. "I need the yellow bowl in there, and we're set."

Jane handed her the bowl, then carried the steaks and vegetables to the table. "Anything else I can do?"

Anna brought the potatoes and salad to the table, sighed, and sank into a chair. "Just sit and eat."

The phone rang just as she clasped her hands to pray. With a sigh of annoyance, Anna started to rise, then settled back into her chair. "The machine will get it." Whoever it was decided to hang up. She had a feeling the *whoever* was Ted.

"Wait." Jane rattled the cubes in her glass. "A toast."

"Hey, yeah." Anna raised her glass. "To my mad cooking skills?"

"And. . ." Jane smiled. "To the best friend anybody could ask for." Her big blue eyes misted. She took a gulp of lemonade. "I'm not going to cry, even though I'm here to help you pack."

Anna quickly spooned corn onto her plate. Another look

in Jane's eyes and her own tears would overflow. "I picked up more cartons today," she said, keeping her goal front and center. Soon, dinners with Jane and their long chats would be a thing of the past. Anna sliced through her steak, swallowing past the lump in her throat. "I just want to get the stored stuff packed and sent to Akron. Stuff I'm not using."

"If your decision is final." Jane shrugged.

If? As though anything or anybody could keep her from God's call again. Anna nodded. "Yep, this time it's final."

Jane stabbed at another piece of steak. "Everything's delicious."

"Thanks. I wonder if they'll let me cook at the orphanage." A smile accompanied the thought. "All those kids. I bet I'll be so busy that one day will run right into the next."

"The kids will love you, cooking or not." Jane poured herself more lemonade. "By the way, have you given Joe notice yet that you're quitting?"

"No, but a month's notice should be fine." Anna smiled. "The truth is, Joe's the type who'll try to put me on a guilt trip. Pressure me for one more month, then another. He's got a way of getting a lot of mileage out of his employees." She laughed. She'd even miss Joe and his quirky ways.

"Speaking of mileage." Jane's brows lifted. "You mentioned on the phone that Joe talked you into a few more meetings with Daniel." She gasped. "I mean *business* meetings."

Anna did her best to ignore Jane's blatant insinuation at romance, but heat crept up her neck. "I know *exactly* what you mean."

Jane snickered. "Good! I wouldn't want to become known for subtlety at this late date in life."

"So Joe talked me into it." Anna relinquished a smile. "Just a couple of meetings with Daniel and that should do it."

"Yep, that should do it all right."

"Would you stop?" Anna forced a laugh to push away another wave of gloom. She'd miss Jane's barbs, too. Chances were she'd never have another friend who understood her as well or could make her laugh at herself.

The phone rang again, shaking Anna's fragile composure. They exchanged glances. "Want me to get it?" Jane stood.

"Go ahead." Anna held her breath with dreaded anticipation.

"Some people hate talking into machines. My mother's one of them. She's probably hunting me down." Jane pulled off her clip earring. "Hello." She pressed the phone closer to her ear, frowned, and covered the mouthpiece. "Traffic noises, breathing."

A spasm of fear soured Anna's stomach. "It's *him*."

"Who?" Jane removed her hand from the mouthpiece. "Whoever this is, you can—"

"No!" Anna jumped to her feet, toppling her chair. "Just hang up!"

Jane set down the phone.

Anna righted the chair. "Forget it. Let's just eat."

"By the way, who is *him*?" Jane sat, then turned her head and eyed the door behind her.

"*Him* is Ted. And don't worry, the door is locked." Anna shoveled mashed potatoes onto her fork while Jane's stare bored a hole through her.

"Ted?" She tapped her fork against the plate. "What's going on? And don't say *nothing*, Anna. You're as pale as a ghost."

"I don't know, just. . . Well, I haven't been answering Ted's calls since Tuesday."

Jane tilted her head. "Mind backing up? Are you telling me Ted's been making obscene phone calls here since Tuesday?"

"See now. . ." Anna inspected the saltshaker, avoiding Jane's worried gaze. "That's why I didn't tell you. You're making a bigger deal of it than it is."

"Bigger than what just happened?" Jane jerked her thumb in the direction of the phone. "If that really was Ted, he's one sick puppy."

Anna's stomach sank. Avoiding Ted, refusing to discuss him, wouldn't make him go away. "Ted showed up here Monday night when Daniel came to pick me up."

"You've got to be kidding!" Jane moved to the edge of her seat. "I can't believe you didn't tell me."

"I didn't want to tell you because—"

"Because you didn't want me to phone Ted and say something *really* mean? Because you're too nice, Anna." Jane grunted. "Well, what happened?"

"Nothing, except. . ." Anna sipped lemonade as the incident blurred through her mind. "I think Daniel was about to deck him."

Jane shot out of her chair, arms raised over her head. "Woohoo! You go, Daniel!" She sat down and popped a piece of steak into her mouth, as if her crazy outburst had never occurred.

Anna stared at her. "It wouldn't have been funny if they'd gotten into a fistfight."

"Of course not, but if it's just jealousy stuff on Ted's part maybe it's not so serious." Jane dabbed the napkin to her lips. "You've gotta love that Daniel, huh?" She stuffed a forkful of salad into her mouth and chewed around her grin. "C'mon, tell me more."

Just jealousy. Anna grabbed hold of the encouraging thought and released a pent-up breath. "It was horrible. Ted had the nerve to introduce himself as my fiancé. Daniel said he wasn't. And it ended with Ted saying, 'See you tomorrow, Anna,' in this creepy voice." She licked her lips, looking at Jane for reassurance. "You know Ted. He's unpredictable, but you don't think he's capable of violence, do you?"

Jane's brows drew together. More than likely, Jane was pondering a nice way to break the bad news. "Capable of violence?"

"Forget it." A shiver ran the length of Anna's spine. "I can't wait to get out of here. I feel like Ted's watching me." A whirl of what-ifs buzzed in her head again. "Am I paranoid or what?"

"No. Ted *is* an insurance investigator. He might have ways—"

Anna nodded. "I thought of that. Like how would he know to show up when Daniel came to get me? Ted's timing was uncanny."

"You really are scaring me." Jane turned to look at the door again. "Do you think he's tapping your phone?"

Anna shivered. "No, of course not. I'm being crazy." She picked up her fork and knife. "He was probably scrounging for a home-cooked meal, is all."

"And probably wanted to reconcile." Jane stabbed her fork into her meat. "You were the best thing to ever cross his path."

Anna gazed at her half-eaten steak, grappling with whether or not to tell all. She looked at Jane. Who else could she tell? "Ted's been leaving messages for two days running. He goes from sweet-talking, 'Anna, I still love you,' to veiled threats in that creepy voice he used in the hallway."

Jane flung down her napkin. "Okay, why don't we call the police?"

She had thought of that herself, but. . . "Because Ted's got friends in high places." Anna shook her head. "Besides, I don't want to incite him."

Jane puckered her lips. "Okay, you may have a point there." She met Anna's gaze. "Let me give this some thought."

Unable to swallow another bite, Anna stood. She scraped her leftovers into the garbage pail. "Ted's not going to hurt me. I'm sure of that."

"I'm glad you're sure." Jane began clearing the table. "But you asked me if I thought Ted was capable of violence. Personally, I wouldn't put it past him."

Anna squirted dish liquid into the sink and turned on the faucet. Hadn't she sensed that about Ted? She didn't need a psychology degree to interpret the devilish look in his eyes, the tone of his voice. "The good news is that I haven't seen Ted since that night in the hall."

"Still, promise you'll let me know if he calls and harasses you again, will you?" Jane picked up a dish towel. "And be careful."

Anna nodded. She'd had enough of this conversation. "I'll clean up. You've got to go into my bedroom and see the flowers Daniel gave me. The petals are just opening."

"The infamous white roses?"

Anna focused on scrubbing the pan. She glanced up long enough to catch a glimpse of Jane's sly grin.

eleven

Daniel stood on the balcony of his apartment, gazing at the avenue fifteen floors below. What did Anna think of living in Manhattan? She said she'd come here on Ted's account. Would she stay? He had so many unanswered questions he couldn't ask under the guise of strictly business.

He tipped back his head and inhaled deeply. Too early for snow, but the October night held the scent of it. Black clouds passed over, revealing a pumpkin-sized moon. Very romantic. Too bad Anna wasn't beside him to share the view. Even though she wouldn't allow romance into her life, he was determined to find a way to change that.

He took another breath of the cold night air and glanced at his watch. "Time to call."

He stepped back into his living room then snapped the glass doors shut. Crossing the wooden floor, his footsteps echoed through the room. There was nothing cozy about his apartment.

He scanned the sparsely furnished space. Barren. And that painting—lines and splotches. Any two-year-old could've done better. What had Paige called it? The minimalist look? With their plans to marry last year, he had let Paige have her way. But it was time for a change.

Daniel eyed the white cordless before picking it up. He punched in the numbers etched in his memory. Anna's phone number. Not surprising, he thought, while he waited. He'd committed everything about her to memory.

"You'd better stop calling here, or we're reporting it to the police!"

Daniel's mind snapped out of his reverie. "Hello? Hello?" He must have the wrong number. "This is Daniel. I want to speak with—"

"Uh-oh." Silence ensued. "Daniel? This is Jane."

"Jane? From the diner? Anna's friend?"

"The way Anna's glaring at me, I highly doubt it." The sound of Jane clearing her throat reached his ear. "Sorry about the mistaken identity."

"Mistaken identity? Has Ted been bothering Anna again?" Irritation burned a path up his chest. He tightened his hand around the phone.

"Um, yes, in fact."

Daniel evaluated her terse reply. "I see. You can't say more because Anna's close by." His mind raced. The last thing he wanted was to add to the growing list of pulling strings behind Anna's back. But Anna had mentioned Jane was a psychologist. Maybe Jane would know if Ted was as dangerous as he appeared. "Jane, I'd like to speak with you about Ted sometime when you're alone." He gritted his teeth. He'd done it again. "Can you remember my cell number if I give it to you?"

"Yes, sure."

Daniel repeated the number twice. "May I speak with Anna now?"

"She's right here."

Daniel dropped onto the black leather sofa. What excuse would she come up with to dodge him? And how long would he have to play at "strictly business"? One comforting thought, she wasn't fawning all over him for his money.

"Anna speaking." She sounded slightly out of breath. A vision flashed through his mind—Anna twisting a lock of her blond hair.

He smiled but summoned his conference voice. "Anna, Daniel Boccini here. I'd like to meet with you tomorrow, about the grant." He heard a distant chuckle—probably Jane— followed by whispers.

"Anna, are you there?"

"Yes, I'm here. Tomorrow should be fine."

A relieved breath whooshed out of him. "Good, good. How about dinner, at seven?"

"Yes."

There was more murmuring in the background. "And Joe gave you the paperwork for me?" he added, in case she reconsidered and called back to cancel.

"Yes, I have the paperwork. But. . ."

Here it comes. "Yes, what is it?"

"I don't like going out on Halloween. Too many weirdoes."

"Ah, well, don't worry, I'll protect you." Daniel shook his head. She was one cautious woman. Must be exhausting to weigh every possibility. Yet the person she should be most worried about, she seemed to be covering for.

"You'll protect. . . ? All right then, I guess that's fine."

"Good night, Anna. Pleasant dreams." Daniel clicked the OFF button on the cordless, settled back on the sofa, and held the phone to his chest. His next step would be to take his parents on a tour of The Center. He needed their approval to release significant funds. What would they think of Anna?

Daniel sat forward. What would Anna think of them? They might intimidate her without meaning to. A bit of uneasiness wormed its way into his thoughts. He stood and snapped the phone back in its cradle. He had to call his parents to make an appointment for them to tour the school.

He crossed the room to the sliding glass doors and stared out. Jane had thought he was Ted on the phone, and she'd threatened to call the police. Daniel's pulse picked up. How was he supposed to protect Anna when she wouldn't confide in him? He sighed. "What are you up to, Ted?"

Daniel snapped off the lights in the living room. He didn't have the answers. But the good Lord did. Time to pray.

In his bedroom, the one corner of the house where Paige hadn't a chance to unleash her creative energy, Daniel knelt on the plush, deep-blue carpet.

"Lord, I'm seeking Your wisdom and direction."

The phone rang. Daniel stayed on his knees, frowning as the answering machine in the living room carried Paige's voice into his bedroom.

twelve

"This weighs a ton!" Anna deposited the carton at her feet.

The in-between room separating her kitchen from her bedroom, and not much larger than a closet, was already crammed to the max. She barely had space to squeeze through the aisle she'd left down the middle.

Anna stepped over the carton and padded to the kitchen sink. She washed the packing grime from her hands, wincing as soap seeped into the tiny cuts on her fingers. All the stuffing, lifting, and tugging had whetted her appetite. She opened the refrigerator door and grabbed the container of plain yogurt. Her gaze shifted to the box that held the last cinnamon bun. Licking her lips, Anna replaced the yogurt on the shelf along with her good intentions. She snatched the bakery box, brought it to the table, and dropped into a chair.

She sighed and sank her teeth into the bun.

Studying one of the four wooden kitchen chairs, she smiled. That had been some feat—outrunning the sanitation truck to rescue them from the curb. As her mother liked to say, "One man's garbage is another man's treasure."

Anna took another bite of the bun. She had so much hope back then—painting the chairs a country blue, stenciling each with patterns of happy white daisies. Life in New York had never amounted to happy white daisies.

She groaned and dropped the bun into the box. Even the lemon yellow she'd painted the kitchen walls shouted her Pollyannaish naïveté. Ted had knocked her off her happy perch when he'd assessed her handiwork. "Different," he managed in his version of a generous compliment.

Anna dampened the dishcloth, swiped the crumbs off the table into the box, and tossed it in the trash. "Well, who cares?"

She gave the cloth a shake and rinsed it out.

The phone jangled. Anna froze. *Oh Lord, don't let it be Ted!* Holding her breath, she listened to her recorded message, followed by the beep.

"Hello, Anna, are you there?"

Her heart paused, then restarted like a pulsating drum. She tossed the cloth on the counter and grabbed the phone. "Hello, Daniel, I'm here." She closed her eyes and drew a deep breath.

"Good, I was hoping I'd find you home."

A smile tugged the corners of her mouth.

"There's been a change of plans."

Her smile vanished. Anna inhaled deeply. How ridiculous—her disappointment. This was only a business dinner. "What kind of change?"

"May I pick you up a half hour later than we planned?" Relief washed through her. He wasn't canceling. "Around seven thirty?"

"Seven thirty?" Anna glanced at the clock, then dropped her gaze to her dust-covered T-shirt and jeans. Why debate? "Great, that'll give me extra time. I'm a mess."

His laughter warmed her like the heat of the sun. "I'm sure you look beautiful as is."

Beautiful? His words were a splash of cold water. "Actually, I don't." Charming and smooth was one thing, but even Ted had never resorted to false flattery.

"If there's a problem, I can—"

"No problem. Seven thirty." A blush warmed her face as silence hung between them. Had she sounded too eager? She hastened to repair the impression. "Seven thirty is better for me, actually."

thirteen

Daniel rang the bell, then smoothed the sticker on the mailbox stating: A. MCCORT—APT 2E. Hearing three short buzzes in response, he stepped outside her building.

What a night for a romantic walk. He squinted up at the dark clouds. Plump droplets of rain hit his face, trickling down the collar of his silk shirt. He shuddered, zipped his suede jacket, and ducked back into the foyer. They'd never find a cab in this weather. Of all nights not to take the limo, but Anna had given him the distinct impression that she didn't like frills. He had considered taking his own car—for about a whole minute. But a new Mercedes fell solidly into the frills category.

Daniel sighed. What was the problem with enjoying God's blessings? He shrugged. Maybe Anna had a point. He never had to learn to appreciate creature comforts. They were always a natural part of his life.

At the creak of the door behind him, Daniel turned. "Ah, there you are, Anna." He smiled, lassoing in the compliment that burned on his tongue. No compliments. No limo. Tonight he'd be the quintessential businessman.

"Yes." Anna raised her hands palms up. "I made it after all."

"And I appreciate it." *I'm-crazy-about-you* had to be written on his face. He turned quickly and opened the door. "Sorry for the inconvenience, but something came up, and. . ." He'd better leave it at that. No need to mention Paige. It would complicate matters and play right into Anna's hands.

"No problem." Anna remained huddled in the doorway under the cement overhang. "Where's the car?"

He bit back a laugh. When would he get it right? "I thought we'd walk. There's a restaurant about two blocks from here." He eyed her thin coat. "Maybe you should take an umbrella?"

"Don't have one. I loaned it to Jane." She smiled like a trooper. "It's not raining too hard. I'll be fine."

In that flimsy coat? Daniel fought to keep irritation off his face. Why couldn't he be himself? Wrap her in cashmere? He reined in his thoughts and nodded her way like a good negotiator. Strategy. Choose his battles and win the war for her heart.

Petite as she was, Anna kept pace with his long strides as he tried to hustle her out of the rain. Daniel extended his arm behind her to draw her near, then yanked it back. Just in time. He stuffed his hands into his jacket pockets as a precaution.

"Where are we eating tonight?" She slanted a gaze up at him.

His determination got lost in her gemstone eyes. His pulse kicked up its rhythm.

"Daniel?"

Her frown brought him back to his senses. He cleared his throat. "Fon-dooz. Do you know the place? It's just around the corner."

"No. Is it new?"

"Pretty much." The restaurant had been around a couple of years, but why risk putting her on the spot, or making her confess again that Ted hadn't taken her anywhere?

Daniel gave her a sideways glance and started unzipping his jacket. "At least put my jacket on over your coat."

"Absolutely not." Anna clamped her cold, wet hand over his. "I'm fine."

He swallowed back his protest and acquiesced. Rain suddenly dropped from the sky harder and faster. Was this a test? He shrugged out of his jacket. "You're getting soaked, Anna." He draped it over her shoulders.

She stopped and looked up at him, eyes guarded. Their gazes locked. She blinked, swallowed, and clasped her hand to her shoulder in a gesture to remove the jacket. "Thanks, but I can't let you—"

Daniel stayed her hand, took hold of her shoulders, and swept her under an awning. He pulled the jacket tighter around her and yanked the zipper upward. Anna stared at him. "That's because you're so stubborn," he said, going for broke.

Anna wriggled her shoulders in a gesture to break free of the jacket, which hung nearly to her knees. "My arms aren't in the sleeves. . .and it's not funny." Even with her head down, he glimpsed a hint of her smile.

"Good! You're trapped!"

Anna jerked her head up. Her hair framed her face like sparkling shards of glass. His breath caught somewhere between heaven and torture. *Just one kiss. . .*

"Trapped, huh?" She suddenly burst into laughter.

Smiling, Daniel scanned her face. He wanted to cup her chin in his hand, lean down, touch his lips to hers. His longing steered his hand to the jacket collar. He lifted it to her neck playfully, trying to keep the humor of the moment.

"We, um. . ." A trace of her smile lingered.

"Are you ready?" Before he did something he'd regret, Daniel put his hand to her back and ushered her out from under the awning. "Let's make a run for it."

They rounded the corner, nearly colliding with a group of masked adults. What was he thinking? She didn't like going out on Halloween night. He could've met with her in his apartment, asked Nicole to be there so Anna wouldn't feel compromised. But he wanted to be alone with her. And what if Paige showed up unannounced again?

He drew Anna closer, veering around the masked marauders. Fon-dooz—candlelight, piano bar, fireplace. He was tempted to apologize in advance for the romantic atmosphere, but they were at the front entrance.

Daniel opened the door and coaxed Anna out of the rain. She turned, and he unzipped her out of his jacket. "Now you're free."

Smiling, Anna rubbed her pretty, slender fingers together. "A fireplace?"

"Yes, and that's our table." Daniel pointed to the booth closest to the flaming hearth.

"So nice." Her eyes, rimmed with dark, wet lashes, sought his. Her smile made his hands itch to pull her into his arms.

He contented himself with removing her coat. A shudder shook her small, slender body. Well, so much for hating luxuries. If there were no taxis to be had, he'd phone Nicole to bring the car around for their trip back home.

Daniel slid into his side of the booth and smiled. Eyeing Anna across the table, he rested his chin on his fist, recalling their private glances in Stavros's diner. In some crazy way, he knew even then that he loved her.

A busboy poured them ice water. "Thank you," Anna said, and without notice, she picked up her bag, fished out a thick envelope, and placed it on the table, leaving no question of her motive for being with him.

He ignored her cue to get down to business. "Have you eaten fondue before?"

"Yes. And this reminds me of"—she glanced around the room—"a place in Memphis where Jane and I used to go to study." She took a sip of water. "Only, there was no piano player."

The man at the baby grand ran his fingers deftly across the keys in a gentle rendition of "As Time Goes By." Anna ran her fingertips along the edge of the envelope.

"Do you like this song, Anna?"

She sat up straighter, her gaze fixed on the pianist. "Very much."

Daniel reached across the table to move the candle. His fingers brushed her knuckles. "Me, too."

Anna jerked back her hand and looked away. Her eyes glistened. Were those tears? If only he could convey his true feelings. Daniel frowned. He wanted to shout, "I'm not playing games," but the timing was wrong.

The background melody, the accompanying lyrics running through his head, Anna's face in the glow of candlelight, combined to melt Daniel's strategy, pushing the song from his heart to his lips. His voice came out softer, huskier than he intended.

"Don't, Daniel." Anna's whispered words sounded forced. She folded her hands on the tabletop. "Stop fooling around."

Daniel sucked in a breath. "I'm not 'fooling around.' " He

leaned back against the seat and managed a smile. "You said you liked the song. I was singing."

"I know, it's just. . ." Anna shrugged. "Well, you know what I mean."

"You don't like my voice?" He crossed his arms and adopted a teasing tone. "I took singing lessons, you know."

"I know." She shook her head. "I mean, I don't know, but you sound as if you did." Anna closed her eyes and took a deep breath. "You have a—a fine voice, Daniel. It's just that. . ." She put the water glass to her lips. "I don't like a lot of ice. It hurts my teeth."

Daniel laughed outright, aware they weren't discussing his singing voice or lack thereof. "If you don't like my voice, Anna, just say so." He was elated she cared enough about him to be nervous. Or was that wishful thinking? "No need to change the subject."

"Look, I'm sorry." She shrugged again. "I'm not very good company actually." She picked up the envelope and held it out to him. "It might be best if you go over this with Joe Palmer."

Daniel studied her intently, measuring the content and inflection of her words. He took the envelope from her hand. "All right, Anna." He set the envelope on the seat beside him to get the reminder of business out of sight. "We have a meal to eat, all right?" The gentle strains of "You Don't Know Me" cascaded through the restaurant and over his soul. Now this is what he should've sung to her.

Anna gave a tremulous smile. "Yes, of course."

A waitress, French beret tilted atop her blond head, appeared at their table wearing a bright smile. "Hi there." With a nod, Daniel acknowledged the perky, young woman. "My name's Kimberly. Can I bring you something to drink before you order?"

Daniel redirected his gaze across the table. "Anna?"

She stopped chewing her lip. "Yes?"

"What would you like to drink?"

"Hmm, what are you having?"

"Hot mulled cider."

"Good choice!" Kimberly cried.

He glanced across at Anna again, but she was staring up at Kimberly with an odd look.

"I'll have the same."

"Okeydokey." The waitress remained tableside. Daniel acknowledged her, his brows raised in question.

"I have a feeling," she said, sweeping a glance over him, "that I know you from somewhere."

Great, just what he needed. And what was the clever response to that? His mind went blank. Anna's fingers gently strummed the tabletop.

Kimberly pressed a pencil to her pouty mouth. "I'll have to think about it, but I'm sure I know you from somewhere." She giggled, pivoted, and pranced away.

Anna stared into her glass of water, maybe hoping the ice would melt as quickly as his hopes. "I, um, should show you something in those papers." Her tone was lighter, leaving him to puzzle over what accounted for the change.

With his gaze steady on her face, Daniel grabbed the envelope off the seat and handed it to her.

Her cheeks colored as she opened the metal clasp, pulled out a stack of pages, and flipped through them. "Yes, here it is."

Daniel stared at the columns of numbers on the page while he tried to think of some way to rescue the moment.

Anna pointed to a spot on the page. "Joe Palmer wanted you to know that the figures for July are blank because—"

"Hi-eee!" Kimberly was back. Daniel braced himself. He'd met her type before. Tenacious. She wouldn't be easily distracted or discouraged from her quest.

She set down their mugs of cider. "Was your picture in a magazine?"

So she'd figured it out. No use denying it. He'd have to take a different tack. "That was quite some time ago."

"Yikes!" She waved her finger at him. "I knew it! I never forget a face."

Daniel skimmed a glance at Anna. She was stuffing the papers back into the envelope, no doubt disgusted by being hit over the head with what she already considered his pretentious lifestyle. He was done for. Out for the count.

A chorus of loud voices drew his attention to the front door. A group of costumed people piled into the room. With a shake of his head, he looked at Anna, but she didn't turn around. Her gaze lingered on the waitress.

Kimberly's head snapped in the direction of the front door. "How adorable! I love Halloween." Daniel cringed as her bright-eyed gaze returned to him. "Later tonight, there's a costume party next door."

He ignored the hint in her voice. "We'd like to order now, please." With his patience wearing thinner, he set his gaze directly on Anna. "Cheese fondue?"

At her answering nod, he gave Kimberly their order, then rested against the seat. What a night this was turning out to be. An outright rejection from Anna, a waitress acting as if he was a celebrity, and a bearded character, baseball cap backwards, sitting at the bar staring at Anna. Not that he could blame the guy.

fourteen

Daniel shifted in his chair. His usual optimism kept him looking for the upside. "Now, you were about to show me something when—"

"When someone from your fan club interrupted." Anna gave a short laugh. "It can wait."

"Yes, Joe can give me the details on—"

"I'm sorry." Her serious gaze rose from the cup to his face. "I can go through the paperwork with you myself." Her voice broke slightly. "I just thought. . . Well, forgive the confusion, okay?"

Daniel shrugged. Interesting. A change of heart? "Forgiven." He cast another glance at the character sitting at the bar. The man's gaze stayed glued to the back of Anna's head.

Kimberly returned, smiling broader than ever. She positioned the fondue pot between them, then lit the can of Sterno under it. She set down a platter heaped with chunks of bread, apples, and pepperoni slices.

"Thank you." Daniel quickly redirected his gaze to Anna.

"You were in one of those magazines about money, right?" Kimberly giggled.

Anna stabbed the short, double prongs of her long fondue fork into an apple slice. Before Daniel had a chance to respond, Kimberly tilted her head in Anna's direction. "Are you his wife?"

Anna's eyes sought his. Without looking at the waitress, she said, "No, I'm not."

"*Kimberly?*" Someone called in the distance. Daniel released an audible breath as she scampered away.

Daniel suggested they pray, and he and Anna lowered their heads. He asked the blessing for their meal; then once more his gaze met Anna's.

"Well, that was something, huh?" She cleared her throat.

"The waitress. . .do you get that often?"

Daniel dunked an apple slice into the pot of bubbling cheeses. "Get what?"

"What just happened with that teenager?" Anna shook her head. "I didn't know you were famous. It must've been difficult for your fiancée to deal with that." Her eyes were direct, finishing her sentence in a question.

Only her serious countenance kept him from laughing. "Believe me, Anna, nothing like that would've fazed Paige. In fact, just the opposite. Paige loved notoriety." He shrugged. "That was only one of our problems, her preoccupation with image."

"Really? Ted would've. . ." She smiled. "Anyway, I guess Paige wasn't jealous like my ex."

He wouldn't bet on that. Daniel looked down to hide his frown. Brenda had tipped off Paige that he was seeing someone at church, and Paige had tried hard to make an uninvited entrance back into his life today.

Daniel tossed off the thought and stepped through the entrance Anna had opened. "Has Ted been harassing you?" He forked a bread cube, swirled it through the melted cheese, and waited. If she'd open up, he wouldn't have to go behind her back to Jane.

"Well. . .yes and no." She frowned. "He calls now and then, leaves strange messages."

Daniel put down the fork and rubbed the muscles knotting at the back of his neck. He stopped and brought his hands to rest flat on the table. "I see." If she detected a hint of his anger, one misplaced word, he sensed it would be the end of the discussion. "Have you asked him to stop?"

"Yes, initially. But I no longer take his calls." She offered a stiff smile. "I'm sure nobody would be stupid enough to leave recorded phone messages if they actually intended to hurt me."

Daniel shot a glance toward the bar at the guy still staring at Anna. A flash of metal shone from the pocket of his denim jacket. Daniel inched over to the opening of the booth. The man's blue eyes blazed with fury as he shifted on the barstool.

Recognition dawned. Beard and cap aside, he knew those eyes as well as Kimberly recognized his magazine photo. His hands clenched into fists. He looked back at Anna.

"Anna, don't take anything for granted. I don't want you to go back to your apartment tonight." He stood and glanced toward the bar area again. The man was gone. Daniel sank back into his seat.

Anna gave him a blank stare, but a worry line formed above her brow. "I don't think it's *that* serious, Daniel."

"Not serious?" At the sound of his voice, she jumped. "I'm sorry." He softened his tone, but a knot of frustration pulsed in his chest. Should he tell her that Ted had been at the bar watching her? Or would he upset her for nothing? It could've been a coincidence. There was the off-chance Ted planned to go next door to the party Kimberly mentioned.

Daniel clamped his hand on her wrist. "Please, pack some things and stay at Jane's or with Nicole tonight."

She smiled. "I'll think about it."

They ate with a wall of silence between them. The food was tasteless to him. Small as she was physically, Anna had a large portion of determination. Coupled with her stubborn streak, he was certain she wouldn't take him up on his offer to stay at Nicole's. Not that she'd turned him down outright—she was too polite for that. But "I'll think about it" most likely meant she had relied on a man once and she wasn't about to do it again. Somehow, he had to convince her to trust him. But how? He tossed options back and forth in his mind and paid the bill.

Daniel hailed a taxi. Anna slid into the car first and huddled near the door, looking totally in her own world.

He stared straight ahead. He may have made a mess of things, and Anna had every right to push him out of her life, but she couldn't stop him from doing everything in his power to protect her from Ted. The guy wasn't just a lover spurned, a man on a mission to win back his fiancée. His angry display in the hallway and his odd behavior tonight at the bar worried

Daniel. Ted had looked determined enough to use every dirty trick in the book.

The cabbie pulled up in front of her building. Daniel paid the fare and without discussion followed Anna into the foyer. "I'll wait in the hall, like before. Just buzz when you get in."

They stood at the base of the stairs. With her eyes cast downward, she smoothed her hand over her hair. "Thanks again for everything."

He ran his finger down her cheek. "As always, my pleasure."

"Well. . ." Anna shrugged and offered her hand. "See you."

Daniel took her hand in his and gave her a reassuring smile. "See you, Anna."

She withdrew her hand and quickly started up the steps. He waited for what seemed an eternity until he heard the sound of the bell.

Daniel looked over his shoulder then crept up the stairs without making a sound.

fifteen

Daniel jolted and swayed in the back seat of a taxicab operated by a Mario Andretti wannabe. As if catnapping on a hallway floor all night hadn't rankled him enough.

Bleary eyed, he stared out the window as the cabbie whizzed in and out of traffic. Mixed with the stale air of the cab hung the faint but distinctive aroma of cat urine.

Daniel grabbed his jacket, held it to his nose, and sniffed. He shook his head. Why think about it? He scowled, forcing further speculation from his mind.

The cab skimmed past a city bus, careened around the corner, and came to a shrieking halt. Daniel lurched and opened his mouth to give the driver a piece of his mind. Too exhausted, he tossed a twenty into the tray. "Keep the change."

He strode through the building lobby and hit the elevator button. All he needed was to bump into somebody he knew. Talk about something the cat dragged in. He kept his head down, recalling his encounter with Anna's next-door neighbor. Poor thing. He nearly scared the elderly woman half to death. He must've looked like a derelict, half-asleep beside Anna's door.

At the sound of pitter-patter over the marble floor, Daniel cringed. Poochie came into view, her owner trailing close behind.

"Good morning." The woman eyed him warily.

Daniel managed a smile. "Morning." He boarded the elevator behind her, noting the unfriendly curl of Poochie's top lip.

He slipped his hands in his pockets and stared straight ahead, longing for the steam of a hot shower, the scent of soap.

Poochie snarled. Daniel inched closer to the door.

"You liked this nice man last time." The woman baby-talked the dog.

Daniel gave Poochie a sideways glance and smiled. The dog

growled and yapped. "It's probably the cat *urr*—the cat," he muttered.

The woman's penciled brows shot up just as the elevator doors popped open. *Safe!*

Daniel cut a right turn and strode straight ahead to his door. The aroma of cedar and orange greeted him. He took an appreciative sniff. *Now this is the way a hallway should smell.* He put the key in the lock, stepped into his apartment, closed the door, and made a beeline to the lavatory.

Home, sweet home. He turned on the hot water faucet full force, stripped off his offensive-smelling clothes, tossing each item atop the hamper.

What had gotten into him? By the light of day, spending the night in Anna's hallway seemed one step from insanity. What if Anna had caught him? How would he have explained his? His obsession with protecting her from Ted? He had no definite proof Ted had a dangerous edge. And it sure would tip his hand. He groaned. "Business relationship. Right!"

After a long, hot shower, Daniel wrapped a towel around his waist and wiped the steam off the bathroom mirror. He checked the setting on his electric razor to maintain his five o'clock shadow. Tilting his head side to side, he decided he could get used to the look. It never occurred to him to go anything but clean-shaven, until Anna hinted that she liked it.

He heard the smothered trill of his cell. He clicked off the shaver, searched through the pile of cast-off clothing, and retrieved the phone from his shirt pocket.

"Yes, hello." He strode into his bedroom and opened the closet doors.

"Hello, Daniel, this is Jane Roberts, Anna's friend."

"Yes, Jane, good to hear from you." He dropped to the edge of his bed.

"You wanted me to call you."

"Yes. I may as well come right out with this. I don't think we have time for subtlety."

Daniel grabbed his suit from the closet and laid it on the bed.

"I've grown. . .fond of Anna."

Silence.

"And her ex-fiancé's behavior has given me pause for concern."

"I absolutely agree with you."

Daniel opened the dresser drawer, took out underclothes and socks, and tossed them on the bed. "I know you're a professional, as well as Anna's friend, and I'd like to discuss some things with you. Would it be possible for us to meet? Soon?"

"I'm on the fly, Daniel, but I'm concerned for Anna, too, and I'm very interested in what you have to say. I'm coming into the city today to see her. Can we talk then?"

Cradling the phone between his chin and shoulder, he slipped into his clothes. "With Anna present?"

"No, no, I don't think that would be wise at this point."

Being cognizant of the fact didn't make hearing Jane's confirmation any easier. "I agree. I'll be finished with my meeting around three thirty. What time is good for you?"

"I have to be at Anna's house at five." Jane's muffled voice told him she'd covered the mouthpiece. "Sorry. . . Can you be at Stavros's diner at four?"

Daniel splashed on a modest amount of cologne. "The diner across from Anna's place? Too close, isn't it?"

"No, she'll be busy cooking. I'm going to her house for dinner."

"I'll see you at the diner at four, all right?"

"Yes, fine." The phone clicked off.

Daniel froze with the cell phone in his hand. What had gotten into him? His good intentions were spilling over into half-truths and deception.

Soon he'd have to confess all.

He dropped onto the blue velvet armchair, tying his laces, taking inventory of his sins of omission. His board had turned down the initial grant proposal from The Center. He should've informed Anna from the get-go. Not to mention how he'd manipulated Joe Palmer into having Anna meet with him.

Maybe he should tell her Paige showed up at his apartment yesterday? Maybe not.

Daniel stood and groaned. What about sleeping beside her door? And now this—a clandestine meeting with Jane.

"Not good." He walked through the apartment to the front door. Frowning, he hefted his briefcase off the chair.

Tomorrow, after church, he'd explain everything to Anna.

❧

Anna placed her Bible on the nightstand. Why hadn't it occurred to her to leave New York earlier than February? She went to her desk, sat, and switched on the laptop. Maybe because she hadn't been spending enough time on her knees seeking the Lord's wisdom.

Anna typed in her password. Aunt Mary would probably love it if she could join her in Haiti sooner rather than later.

Her e-mail messages appeared on the screen. Anna scanned them quickly. "Nothing important."

She started a post to her aunt.

Dear Aunt Mary,
*   As you know, I'm scheduled to arrive in Haiti mid-February, but there's no reason I should stay in New York till then. I need to give my boss a month's notice, otherwise, how does mid-December sound? Could you ask the director?*

Anna stared at the blinking cursor. Was December even soon enough? Her gaze dropped to the right hand corner of the computer screen. 4:17 p.m. Time to start dinner.

*   I hope you're doing well. I miss you. I visit the Precious Children Web site often. The kids are beautiful. I can't wait to get there but I'm afraid I'll want to adopt all of them myself.*

Anna smiled. Her aunt had assured her that seeing the children placed with loving adoptive parents could be just as rewarding as adopting. But each time she looked at their photos, she grew more skeptical.

I know you have some difficulty getting through to me because of electrical problems, but write when you can. I look forward to hearing from you. Soon!

Your loving niece,
Anna

Anna snapped off the laptop, went to the kitchen and removed the plate of chicken cutlets from the refrigerator. She couldn't ask for a better friend than Jane. She was willing to take the train in from Queens to Manhattan to help her do more packing.

She breathed a sigh of relief and cracked an egg into the bowl. She thanked the Lord Jane had promised to stay overnight. After what Mrs. O'Leary had told her about the man outside her door, how could she stay in this apartment alone?

Anna whipped the eggs then poured breadcrumbs onto a plate. Maybe Jane would attend church services with her tomorrow. She dipped the cutlets into the egg, praying while she prepared their meal.

sixteen

Daniel stood on the curb in front of his store and hailed a taxi. Something told him meeting Jane so close to Anna's apartment wasn't a good idea. At least the conference at his store had been fruitful. Another acquisition should make his parents happy. Now for the conference with Anna's best friend.

He glanced at his watch. 4:10. Hopefully, Jane would wait.

After a stop-and-go ride, he asked the cabbie to drop him off around the corner from the diner. He paid the fare, hopped out of the car, and dipped his head, thinking of Anna standing at her window.

He pulled open the door of Stavros's diner and caught sight of Jane in a booth in the back. She glanced up, smiled, and waved as he walked toward her. She held out her hand before he sat down.

Daniel shook her hand. "Sorry I'm late." He dropped his briefcase on the seat and slipped into the booth.

Jane shrugged. "No problem. I'm always late." She glanced around. "I'm glad you made it."

Daniel nodded. If Anna did catch them together, how would he explain away their good intentions?

The waitress came to the table. Daniel ordered a cup of tea. Jane sucked soda through a straw in a giant-sized glass. Her gaze stayed steady on his face.

"Where do we start?" Daniel folded his hands on the tabletop.

Jane tilted her head. "Why don't you tell me what has you concerned for Anna?"

"All right. Last night, I took Anna out to dinner a few blocks from here." He shook his head as if to clear the image. "Ted was sitting at the bar, disguised in a beard, gaping at Anna like—"

"Oh no!" Jane's head snapped back. "Anna never told me."

"Anna didn't see him. And I didn't want to frighten her, so I suggested she stay at my cousin's house after she mentioned Ted's phone calls."

"I've got worse news." Jane scanned the diner then returned her gaze to him. "Anna knows for sure Ted's stalking her."

"How?"

"Her next-door neighbor caught him lurking outside her door around four this morning."

He drew a breath. "Oh no."

"Oh yes!" Jane's eyes narrowed. "I'm sleeping over tonight, but what about all the other nights?"

The waitress slid the cup of tea in front of him. "Thank you." Now what? Tell Jane the truth? "How did Anna's neighbor know it was Ted?"

Jane fell back against the seat. "She didn't. She just said 'some man.' But who else would it be?"

"You know this city. It could've been a. . .vagrant."

Jane stared at him. "You said yourself Ted was in the restaurant last night." She looked straight into his eyes. "I'm not buying that a vagrant happened by Anna's door."

"You're right." Daniel shrugged off his discomfort. He took a sip of tea. "Do you have any idea what Ted wants of Anna?"

She stared at him for a moment, then smiled, as if she'd decided to trust him. "Ted's a classic case." She snorted. "He may not want Anna, but his ego won't let anybody else have her."

A band of tension tightened around his chest. Daniel scooted to the edge of his seat. "You're saying another man's attention put Anna in danger?"

Jane grinned. "Not another man's—*yours*. And not to change the subject, but Anna should see you now. We thought you looked drop-dead handsome in jeans. You look fantastic in a suit."

Daniel felt a smile come to his face. "Anna said that?"

"No." Jane's grin widened. "Anna wouldn't *say* something like that, but I know she thought it."

"I guess that's better than nothing." Daniel grinned back. "Thanks for the crumb. It's been slim pickings."

Jane laughed then drained the glass of soda. She held it up, rattled the ice. The waitress gave her a thumbs up.

He held back a laugh. From their mannerisms, to their speech, Jane and Anna were so different. What could they possibly have in common?

Jane sighed, suddenly sobered. "Back to the subject. The truth is, Ted can't handle rejection, and that scares me. He's the one who cheated, but he blames Anna. He has to. Ted's personality type never accepts responsibility for one's own actions. So he's told himself, and of course, Anna, that his affair came about because she stood by her convictions and refused to be physically intimate with him."

Daniel nodded slowly, as though Anna had apprised him of these details. So his first impression of Anna was correct—she was sincere through and through about serving God.

The waitress came with another soda. Jane took a sip and again zeroed her gaze in on him. "Ted's been calling her day and night. Leaving all kinds of coaxing messages. 'We belong together, Anna.' And things like, 'I need you, and you need me.' Which tells me that same type of man would blame the woman when the relationship ended, even if it was *his* fault."

Daniel stared into the teacup. "Ted can't take no for an answer." But then, neither could he. At least, he didn't want to.

"That's right. And last night was the final straw." Jane grunted. "Imagine, camping out beside her front door! How desperate can a man get?"

"Desperate?" Daniel frowned. "That's pretty harsh. Love can make men do very stupid things."

Jane tossed him a saucy grin. "Like what?"

Daniel shot her a look and loosened his tie. "Like sleeping beside Anna's door all night."

Her gaze lingered on his face. "Well, it's not normal."

"Neither are the circumstances!" Daniel scowled. "Look, I'm not minimizing. . . I agree with you. Ted's phone messages are not to be taken lightly. And when I saw him sitting at the bar last night. . ." A surge of anger shot through him.

"So what should we do?"

"I'll have a talk with Ted. If he won't leave Anna alone after that, I'm going to the police."

"Anna doesn't want the police involved. She thinks Ted will stop bothering her. . .eventually."

"He won't go away." Looking at Jane now, the sincerity in her eyes, he could easily fathom the depth of their friendship. "First, he shows up when I come to get Anna. Did she tell you?"

Snorting a laugh, Jane nodded. "That was funny. I heard you were going to deck him."

He wanted to laugh with her, but the weight of the situation bore heavy on him. "What does Anna have against contacting the police?"

"She thinks it'll incite him. Anna didn't know until she moved to New York, but Ted's family is pretty sketchy."

"Sketchy?" He shook his head. "As in. . . ?"

Jane stabbed the ice cubes in her glass. "Ted's family knows people. That's how they got him his job."

Daniel's fingers tightened around the cup. If he had to sleep in Anna's hallway every night, so be it. "Jane, there's something I have to tell you."

She dropped the straw and straightened. "Shoot."

"It was me. I'm the one who camped out beside Anna's door last night." He looked her straight in the eye, prepared for her to pronounce him certifiable.

"Too much!" Jane's loud voice returned.

"I know what you think, but—" He stopped speaking at the sound of her laughter. "You already guessed it, didn't you? Do you think I'm crazy?"

"Yes, I guessed it, and yes, I think you're crazy!" She shook her head, still laughing. "But that's the kind of crazy I live for. Who said chivalry is dead?"

Daniel studied her expression. She and Anna were as unalike as burlap and silk. But she got it. "Then you know my intentions are good?"

"Absolutely." Jane's expression grew serious. "I just don't know how long you can go on sleeping in Anna's hall."

"You're right." Pausing, he tried to collect his thoughts. "You're staying over at Anna's house tonight. I guess we'll figure it out from there."

"One day at a time." Jane nodded. "It's not as if we can report Ted to the police for showing up in the same restaurant as you and Anna."

"Right, but one more incident and I *will* have a talk with him." He looked up at her, wanting to probe for more. Not about Ted this time.

"Give Anna some time," she said, as if she'd read his mind. "She's been through a lot."

"I understand that, but I intend to prove to Anna that I'm worthy of her trust."

Jane propped her hand under her chin. "You're an enigma, you know?"

"Why?" He smiled. "Because I know what I want?"

"No, but say there was a lineup of eligible bachelors. If I had to choose a guy for my best friend, he wouldn't be a wealthy city boy." She grinned. "You are wealthy, aren't you?"

"Well, um, I—"

"Yep, you are." Jane laughed. "Anyway, I'd choose a quiet country pastor or a missionary."

"I guess that's bad news for me." His heart sank like a rock.

Jane shook her head as if she'd said too much. She glanced at her watch. "Whew, I better get going." She rose abruptly. "Anna's making chicken cutlets tonight."

Daniel looked up at her. "Thanks for everything."

"Thank you for loving my friend enough to care so much."

"Better hurry."

Jane clapped a hand to his arm. "Wish you were coming, too."

"We're not expecting miracles, yet."

"Bye, Daniel." She started strutting off.

Daniel turned. "Jane?"

She stopped and swung around. "Yes?"

"Why don't you go to church with Anna tomorrow?"

"Maybe." Smiling, Jane tilted her head. "We'll see."

Resting his elbows on the table, Daniel dragged his hands through his hair. He might as well order dinner here.

He took his cell phone from his pocket and dialed his parents' house. At least he could share the good news that he'd acquired the new premises. The phone rang once. He punched the OFF button. Something had zapped the excitement from his accomplishment.

The waitress slapped the check on the table. "Will there be anything else, hon?"

His appetite disappeared as well. "No, that's it." He tossed a tip on the table and went to the register to pay the tab.

He loved Manhattan—his lifestyle, too, to be completely honest. And now he felt like apologizing for all of it.

Daniel paid the bill and walked outside. He glanced up at Anna's building. How could he blame Ted for pursuing her? Though he'd never trust the guy alone with Anna. He intended to have a face-to-face with that character.

He turned the corner and strode towards Third Avenue. What had Jane tried to tell him? A pastor? A missionary? If Anna needed a man in ministry to make her happy, he definitely didn't qualify.

Daniel hailed a taxi. He hopped into the cab, gave his address, and took out his cell. He wasn't a pastor or a missionary. But didn't the Lord need businessmen, too? He could afford to donate large sums of money. That had to count for something.

He dialed his parents' house again, and his father answered.

He tried to sound excited about the new store acquisition then segued into a conversation about The Center. Sweating out their ambiguity over donating to a secular cause, he eventually convinced them to see the school before making a decision.

"That's that," he whispered. He'd appear the biggest fool if they ultimately refused the funds. And that would be the end of his excuse to see Anna.

seventeen

Awaking to the buzz of the alarm clock, Anna rolled onto her side with a groan. She reached for the clock on the nightstand, rapping her knuckles against a hard surface.

"Ouch!" Anna sat upright. She was on the floor mat instead of the bed. Jane slept over, she suddenly recalled.

Shoving at the quilt, she discovered the clock at the foot of the mat and snapped off the alarm. She craned her neck to see Jane, sleeping soundly on the four-poster, snoring.

Anna smiled. Though it had taken a lot to convince Jane to take the bed instead of the mat, Jane easily agreed to attend church with her this morning. A sweet answer to prayer.

Anna stood up in the darkened room, turned to the window, drew aside the curtain, and lifted the venetian blind slat. The sooty pane revealed a city still asleep. One noticeable sign of life came from the flashing green neon sign of Stavros's diner.

Frowning, Anna released the blind slat. If only she hadn't been in the diner that fateful Saturday morning, licking her wounds in public, vulnerable to anybody who would've walked into her life—let alone God's gift to womankind.

Anna tiptoed over the creaky floor and hefted the Bible from the dresser. Stepping around the cartons in the next room, she made her way into the kitchen and set her Bible on the table.

She carried the glass coffeepot to the sink, turned on the cold-water faucet, and groaned. Even Jane had acted all swoony when she'd seen Daniel standing at the cash register. Maybe her own response to him hadn't been over-the-top.

Anna grimaced. Why lie to herself? Smack-dab in the middle of mourning over her breakup with Ted, she'd felt the current of a thousand-volt jolt when her eyes met Daniel's. And after Daniel walked out of the diner, for a dangerous split second, she wondered if God's mate for her had disappeared forever.

She shuddered, snapped back the faucet handle, poured water into the coffeemaker, and slammed down the lid. She had to face facts. The more she tried not to like Daniel, the more she did.

Anna peeled back the plastic cover from the coffee can, inhaling the rich aroma as she scooped grinds into the basket. Speculating that a total stranger in a diner might be her future husband testified to her post-Ted pathetic condition.

Anna flicked the switch on the coffeemaker. "Oh boy, I think I lost count."

"Talking to yourself again?"

With a shiver, she spun toward a yawning Jane. "Hey, you're up early."

"That bed of yours is comfy." Jane dropped into a kitchen chair. "I slept like a dead dog."

A dead dog? Where did Jane get such expressions? "Glad you slept well." Anna eyed the coffee machine. "Because we might be drinking mud this morning."

"I'm guessing that's what you lost count of? Scoops?" Jane grinned. "Maybe you're in love?"

"Could be, but"—Anna went to the cabinet, grabbed two coffee mugs off the shelf, and brought them to the table—"I'm *not* in love." She was on the rebound from Ted, is all. She might love the idea of being in love, but. . . "I saw something interesting on one of those daytime talk shows the other day." Anna set the creamer on the table beside the sugar bowl.

Jane slanted her a sleepy-eyed glare. "What's that got to do with anything?"

Anna sat and flipped open her Bible, ignoring Jane's smirk. "There was this psychologist on." Maybe she should just let sleeping dogs lie. She shook her head.

"Hello? I'm listening."

Too late to backpedal, Anna shrugged. "Anyway, this psychologist said some people, especially women, run from one relationship to another." She met Jane's curious gaze and cleared her throat. "Because women are looking to fill their love tanks. So the first guy who comes along—"

Jane laughed. "Good try, Anna!" She stood, snickering. "And you want to know if *you're* one of those women?"

Anna grunted. "I knew I shouldn't have told you!"

"I'm sorry for laughing." Jane wagged her head. "I understand the concept, but it doesn't apply in this case. You weren't exactly scouring the globe for Mr. Right. Not after Ted! You and Daniel—it just happened." She swiped her coffee mug off the table. "Hey, can I pour myself some java while this thing is still brewing?"

"Yes." Anna looked away from her, miffed. "It's got a safety valve."

"Just like you," Jane muttered.

What did Jane mean? *It just happened.* Nothing at all had *happened.* Pushing Jane's remark out of her head, Anna looked at her open Bible and began reading.

Jane shuffled back to the table, sat down, and splashed cream in her coffee.

Anna continued to read the Bible, ignoring the clink of Jane's ring against the cup—her habit of signaling she wanted to talk. Her dear friend could *tap-tap* all she wanted, but she wouldn't be drawn into another hilarious discussion about such a serious topic.

Jane took a sip of coffee and whistled. "Whew! You're in love all right."

Anna laughed without wanting to. "That strong?"

Jane took another gulp despite her complaints. "I bet I know what you were dreaming about when you shoveled in those extra scoops." She cleared her throat. "Or should I say, *whom* you were dreaming about?"

Anna stared at Jane's face—a picture of wide-eyed innocence. "Okay, I admit I was thinking about *him*." She folded her hands on the Bible. "Thinking how weak and foolish a woman can be after she finds out her fiancé has been unfaithful."

"Interesting. Now we're getting somewhere."

Anna picked up her coffee mug and went to the counter.

She poured herself half a cup of the madwoman brew, returned to the table, and sat, raising her chin a notch. "You should be proud of me. You warned me about being naïve. I'm finally getting it."

Jane snorted. "Yeah, but you're practicing on the wrong man."

As she stirred cream and sugar into her coffee, Anna refocused on the book of Ruth. Though the last thing she needed was to read about the compassionate, wealthy Boaz who fell hard for Ruth the moment he laid eyes on her. *Next page.*

Jane resumed strumming her fingers. "What are you reading?"

As much as she was still irritated, she took the bait. "A story about a widow named Ruth. She meets a man—"

"Hey, I know that story!" Jane perked up in her chair.

Anna frowned. "You know the story of Ruth and Boaz?" Jane had never before mentioned reading the Bible. Strange.

Anna took a sip of coffee and shuddered. *Poison.*

"My dad used to read Bible stories to me." Jane smiled. "I was just a kid, but I guess some of the characters stuck with me."

"I'm sorry, I didn't mean to bring up—"

"Don't be." Jane stood and carried her cup to the sink. "As you know, my dad died before I was six. It's not like it happened yesterday."

Poor Jane. She didn't need the reminder. Anna closed the Bible. More romance talk should cheer her. "So what did you think of the Ruth and Boaz story?"

"Love at first sight, wasn't it?"

She had to give Jane that much. "I'll say."

A sneaky grin crossed Jane's face. "On both their parts, right?"

Easy for Ruth. She was fully confident Boaz was God's man for her. "In those days, people didn't date as we know it." Anna stood and snatched up her Bible and coffee mug.

Jane frowned. "You don't believe that love at first sight is for the twenty-first century?"

Love at first sight—a troublesome thing. Anna placed her cup in the sink. Clasping the Bible to her chest, she sighed. "I see what you're getting at, but I thought I knew Ted once and. . ."

Worse, she'd prayed hard and believed the Lord gave her the go-ahead with Ted. "Anyway, it doesn't make any difference at this point."

Jane crossed her arms. "I wish I could convince you that you're making a big mistake distrusting Daniel."

"I'm not saying I *distrust* him—exactly." Anna pressed the Bible closer to her thudding heart. "But you saw Daniel, what? One time? For about a whole minute? Good looks and money never influenced *you* when it came to dating."

"I can't say"—Jane met her gaze and held it—"there are things I can't explain."

Anna's shoulders relaxed at Jane's admission. Chasing rainbows was well and good once in a woman's lifetime. Twice would be hideous. She pasted on a smile. "Daniel makes a stunning first impression is all." A half-truth, if she'd ever told one. She'd sat across from him, starry-eyed and breathless, in the church's fellowship hall. Daniel, standing in the doorway of her office with the lunch he prepared for her, the almost kiss. . .

Anna's stomach clenched. "I've got to take a shower."

"Okay, but remember, you promised I could do your hair and makeup today."

"Yep." Anna hurried from the room to hide whatever emotion showed on her face. She set her Bible back on the dresser. She snapped the bathroom door closed and released a deep breath. If allowing Jane to give her a makeover was all it took to get her to church, so be it. But one more attempt at playing matchmaker, and she'd. . .

Anna adjusted the water temperature in the shower. She didn't know what she'd do, short of telling Daniel that her friend was a nutcase.

Lifting her face to the spray of hot water, Anna closed her eyes, envisioning Daniel's concerned expression as she told him she deemed Jane certifiable.

Anna clamped her hand over her mouth, smothering a giggle.

eighteen

Wearing a smile—and feeling every inch an over-painted dime-store doll—Anna held open the church door for Jane.

"You look great," Jane said when she reached the top step.

Swallowing a sarcastic retort, Anna simply nodded. Together, they approached the inner doors to the chapel. "Where's Daniel?" Jane whispered solemnly.

"*Shh.*" Anna summoned her most serious tone. "We're not here to see—" At the tap on her shoulder, she swung around, meeting Daniel's dark gaze head-on. She stiffened, waiting for the full effect of Daniel in his dark blue suit to pass. *Oh Lord, what's wrong with me?* "Good morning."

"Good morning, Anna."

Jane nudged her before shaking Daniel's proffered hand. "Nice to meet you. . .again." Another rib jab from Jane prompted Anna to inch over.

"And you, Jane." He switched his focus, a smile crinkling the corners of his eyes. "Good to see you, Anna."

Basking in his powerful presence, Anna tried to strike a deliberately casual pose, leaving her struggling to tuck her mousse-filled hair behind her ears.

"You look lovely." Daniel leaned forward a bit, as if in a bow.

"Doesn't she?" Jane tilted her head. "She looks like a young Meg Ryan, don't you think?"

Anna shot Jane a tight-lipped smile. If only it were possible to strangle her and then bring her back to life.

"Yes. But Anna is beautiful in her own right."

Heat singed the tips of her ears. "I don't look like Meg Ryan by any stretch," she directed to Jane then turned to Daniel. "And beauty is in the eye of the beholder." She felt her face flame crimson. "I—I mean, beauty is highly subjective."

94

Smiling down into her eyes, Daniel placed his hand over his heart. "Yes, it is. Let's find a seat, shall we?"

"Sure thing," Jane exclaimed in cheerleader fashion before Anna could speak. "And, Daniel, you remind me of Andy Garcia." She snickered.

Daniel quirked a brow and smiled. Anna looked away from him, disheartened that she'd allowed their playfulness to get the better of her.

Jane scooted behind her, nudging Anna into the pew so she'd be seated next to Daniel. Anna opened her mouth to protest, sighed, and turned around in defeat. Okay, she could afford to lighten up a bit. She sat, pulled her Bible out of her bag, and set it atop her lap.

Daniel pointed to the Bible. "May I see that?"

Anna slapped her hand flat against the leather cover. "Why?"

He laughed. "You do quite a bit of note-taking in church. Just curious which scriptures are your favorites."

Anna looked down at the worn book. How could she refuse the innocent request? Her stomach somersaulted. She handed it to him. The verses in Genesis. . .underlined. Highlighted in bright pink! The notes in the margin!

She held her breath. *Lord, I'm begging you, please don't let him turn to Genesis.* Facing forward, she slid a glance to her left to see where he was reading. His finger moved along a highlighted passage. "Nice," he muttered. "I love this one, too."

Anna looked at him as if she'd been absorbed in a totally unrelated thought. "Which one?"

"Jesus loved us before we first loved Him." Daniel smiled. "An awesome kind of love, huh?"

Anna blinked quickly and nodded. "Yes, unconditional love."

Daniel continued flipping through her Bible. He stopped and turned the book sideways, nodding as he read. He hummed a throaty sound of discovery. "Ah, look at this." Anna's stomach swished like a washing machine. "This is beautiful, Anna."

With a cursory glance at the Bible, she felt the color siphon from her face. Genesis chapter two—all her dreams exposed to him in splashy, little-girl pink!

Daniel's eyes met hers. "Have you found the man God has for you?" The earnestness in his expression begged an honest answer, but she couldn't speak.

She swallowed the golf-ball-sized pain in her throat and glanced away. "The service is about to start."

Daniel handed her the Bible.

Jane elbowed her. "Everything okay?" she whispered as the music started.

Anna nodded and rose with the congregation. *Is everything okay?* She wanted to scream a desperate *"No!"* If Jane weren't beside her, blocking the opening of the pew, she would bolt out the church doors.

She had to face facts. Some sort of character deficiency made her capable of even considering. . .

No! Not again. If her fairy-tale imagination led her to believe she'd seen love in Daniel's eyes, she need only remind herself of her history and her blind stupidity with Ted. If she messed up again, she'd not likely get a third opportunity to go to Haiti. She'd be stuck in Manhattan forever. Alone.

Anna stared up at the white screen. What beast beat within her breast, drawing her away from her good intentions time and again? She closed her eyes, refusing the tears. *Lord, speak to my heart. I need answers.*

But she knew the answer.

The greater the distance she put between herself and Daniel, the faster she'd get her life back on track.

I acknowledge my weakness, Lord. Forgive me, and please, give me a tangible sign.

❧

They stood outside the church. "How about it, Anna?" With Jane in his corner, Daniel summoned the boldness to invite them to his place for brunch.

Anna glanced at her watch again. "I don't think so." She looked at Jane. "Remember the stuff we had to do?"

"Stuff?" Jane crinkled her nose. "What stuff?"

Daniel gestured to the limo. "Come on, Anna, Nicole is waiting. She'd love to spend some time with you." And he'd love it even more. He looked at Jane. "With both of you. Nicole's new to Manhattan and wants to make friends."

Anna bit her lip and shrugged. "I appreciate the invitation, I really do, but there's no way—"

"Why not?" Jane grabbed Anna's arm and gave her a little shake. "Whatever *stuff* we need to do can wait till later."

Daniel restrained a smile. He'd certainly found an ally in Jane. "Good." He strode to the car and held open the door.

Anna hesitated before sliding in without giving him as much as a glance.

Daniel turned, eyeing Jane as she stood frozen on the sidewalk, her hands pressed to her cheeks. "Oh! I just remembered. I have a paper to write on a patient study!"

"I see." Daniel stifled an appreciative smile. "You can't join us then?"

Jane waved. "No, sorry." She pivoted and wound her way through the church crowd.

Daniel hopped into the car and closed the door quickly to prevent the elusive butterfly from escaping.

"Can you believe Jane?" Anna shook her head as the limo pulled away.

"Wonderful that Jane decided to join us in church." He assessed Anna from the corner of his eye. She sat with her hands clasped tight around one knee. He didn't need to be a body-language expert to know she wanted nothing to do with him right now. Loosening his tie, he searched his mind for an icebreaker. "So, Anna, what did you think of the service?"

"I enjoyed it."

At least he had her talking. Her floral scent floated over him. Was it jasmine? He forced his mind back to the topic. "Pastor Meyers is something else, isn't he? Transparent. A what-you-see-is-what-you-get kind of guy."

Anna turned to the side window, leaving Daniel to stare at the back of her pretty blond head. "True. Wouldn't it be nice if you could say that about most people?"

His heart sank. If Anna meant the barb for him, it worked. She didn't trust him. There went his plans for confessing his sins of omission. Not today. Maybe not ever. Daniel cleared his throat. "Were you listening in church?"

Anna jerked back around, sending wisps of hair across her cheek. Struck with the temptation to kiss her, Daniel clasped his hands loosely in front of him. She tilted her chin. "Of course I was listening."

He swore he heard her teeth grinding together. "The Bible says man doesn't know his own heart. How can we expect to know another man's heart?"

She looked at him, eyes wary. "Okay. . ."

"All I'm saying. . ." He lost his train of thought. Would she always want to catch him in something? "I'm saying it's unreasonable to expect most people to be transparent."

Anna fiddled with her purse chain. "So then, we agree."

Despite the undercurrent of irritation in her voice, he couldn't help but smile. "I'd say, all too often, we're not aware of our deepest motives. How can we always be transparent?"

Anna's eyes widened. "Exactly!" Her voice rang with victory. "That makes the case for being wary of trusting anyone too easily."

Checkmate! While Daniel formed a rebuttal, her smile vanished and her shoulders sagged, dampening his frustration. "Jesus said we'd know people by their fruits, Anna."

"I know." She continued twisting the chain on her purse. "And how do *you* interpret that?"

Yes, she was determined to think the worst of him. "It means a good tree bears good fruit, and a bad tree, well. . . You'll know good people by the way they talk, act, treat others. I love that simple truth. Some people read into things far too deeply for their own good."

Anna stared straight ahead. Daniel gazed out the car window. She had him doubting himself, though he'd treated her as best as he knew how. He'd withheld certain information from her, but he meant only to show her love and kindness.

The glass divider slid open. "Daniel, I go to garage?"

"Yes, Nicole, you'll join us for brunch."

Facing the window, Anna looked up. "Nice building." Her voice was cool.

The car descended into the dim garage, and Nicole swung into his designated parking slot.

Daniel drew a deep breath. He shouldn't have brought Anna here. Not yet. This building, his apartment, would be an affront to her sensibilities. Him and his impatience.

When they reached his front door, Daniel said a prayer and slipped the key into the lock. He opened the door and waved. *"Benvenuto alla mia casa."*

Anna halted, turned, and looked up at him. "Oh, I love Italian. Does that mean welcome?"

He'd finally done something right. "Yes." Daniel returned her smile, but Anna turned and trailed Nicole into the living room. Unbuttoning her coat, she glanced around. "You've got so much space! It's lovely."

"Thank you." Daniel took her coat. "Sit down, please. Make yourselves at home."

Anna meandered to the sliding glass doors. "I've never seen the city from this high up. May I go out on the terrace?"

Daniel smiled. This might turn out well after all. "Yes, of course." He strode to the doors, unsnapped the lock, and opened the door. He draped Anna's coat over her shoulders and followed her outside.

"I go to the kitchen," Nicole chimed.

He signaled to her with a wave. "Yes, fine."

Anna clamped her fingers on the railing atop the cement enclosure. "I imagine this view is awesome at night. All the lights. . ."

"Yes." He couldn't help but brush a strand of her windblown hair from her cheek. She remained still. He was grateful she didn't shrink back from him. "One evening I'll make dinner for you, and you can see the view at night."

Anna lifted her gaze to his, drew her coat tighter around her shoulders, and took a step toward him. Not wanting to ruin the magic of the moment, Daniel ignored the ringing phone, inclined his head, and leaned in closer.

The answering machine clicked on. "Please leave a message."

Anna lifted her face to his. Daniel trailed his fingers under her chin.

The *beep* sounded. "Daniel? This is Paige, Daniel. Are you there?"

Anna drew back, her face flushed.

Daniel opened his mouth to speak.

"I'm cold." Anna turned and stepped into the living room.

Daniel followed then snapped the door shut. *Paige!*

Nicole set down a tray of snacks on the coffee table, turned, and dashed back into the kitchen.

"I assumed you'd be home from church by now, Daniel," Paige continued speaking in her typical, stomping-her-spoiled-little-feet voice. "But I'll try you later." The sound of her breathing followed. "It was great seeing you Friday. You're as irresistible as ever. Smooch." She giggled. *Click.*

Daniel slipped his hands into his pockets and glanced at Anna. Her faint smile told him nothing. "Any tips on how to handle an ex who won't give up?"

Anna's pretty brows drew together. "I don't know. Ted's been quiet lately." She lifted one shoulder. "Then again, I don't date him anymore."

Her words hit him like stones. How did she manage to pummel him with such a sweet voice? Daniel shook his head. "I don't date Paige either, but. . .well, you know how it can be." He shrugged. "May I take your coat?"

"Sure." Anna handed it to him with an outstretched arm clearly meant to keep him at a distance.

"Please have a seat," Daniel called over his shoulder on his way to the foyer. He opened the closet door and groaned. Leave it to Paige. He could only imagine what Anna would make of the innuendo.

Irresistible! Daniel slammed the closet door then headed to his bedroom. He swiped off his tie, removed his cufflinks, and tossed them on the dresser.

His pulse pounded with irritation. He had a good mind to march into the living room, tell Anna everything, sweep her into his arms, and kiss her.

And kiss her.

Yes, that would be a brilliant move—explain to a supposed business associate why Paige was phoning him. He would embarrass Anna with the tawdry details. Paige, draping herself all over him to where he had to peel her arms from around his neck. Daniel shuddered. To think he'd almost married her.

On his way back to the living room, the kitchen door swung open. Nicole grabbed his arm and reeled him in, pressing her finger against her lips.

Daniel frowned. *Now what?*

nineteen

Anna stared out the car window. She'd prefer to be in a taxi. Alone. But Nicole had insisted on driving her back home.

Surviving the four-hour brunch intact had been a small miracle. After hearing Paige's phone message, her first instinct was to bolt. But she stayed and pasted on a smile, aware that her status as business acquaintance gave her no right to hurt feelings just because Daniel got a phone call from his ex-fiancée.

Anna forced her thoughts to the high points of the brunch. There were moments when she'd felt blissful.

Still, there'd be no more wavering. Daniel had told her his relationship with Paige was over. Yet they were still seeing one another. In church, she'd asked God for a sign. Paige's phone call had set her free. She could leave for Haiti now with a clear head and heart. If she ever again allowed herself to be deluded into thinking Daniel was the one for her, she'd remember his deception. Mercifully, Daniel would never discover she'd entertained the embarrassing notion.

She should be relieved. Happy. So why wasn't she?

Sweet Nicole had put out a banquet for them. Daniel must've preplanned the brunch, though she was no longer interested in his motives. Or maybe he stockpiled food for all the women he entertained. He was definitely smooth and practiced.

Tipping back her head, Anna closed her eyes. Behind her lids lingered the uninvited image of Daniel.

Mostly she tried to avoid eye contact with him throughout the brunch. Except for one unguarded moment when she ventured a glance his way and her mind disengaged from her speeding heart. As if Daniel had detected her thoughts, he met her gaze and held it, and for a second she imagined she saw love in his eyes.

Anna's eyes moistened. Daniel had given her the impression he liked her. Hadn't he? He stood so close on the terrace, she thought he might kiss her. Or had she imagined there was more between them than business?

Anna twisted her hands in her lap. She could handle spending time with Daniel on a purely professional basis. Tomorrow she'd meet with Daniel and his parents.

Anna's stomach dipped. *Why did you ever allow me to meet him, Lord? Why?*

She burrowed deeper into her coat. Thank God for His intervention. She could've been another conquest in the life of another playboy. Not a sexual conquest; the Lord had given her the grace to cherish her purity.

The car stopped at her building. Anna surveyed the interior of the limo for what she sensed would be the last time.

❧

Where are you, Nicole? Daniel sank further behind the wheel of his car. All he needed was for Anna to catch him out here.

Of course, she wouldn't. She had never seen his Mercedes. Not willing to take chances, he lifted his jacket collar to conceal his face.

At least he'd gotten Anna to agree to meet with him and his parents at The Center tomorrow.

But that miserable phone call! Daniel's hands tightened on the steering wheel. If Anna had gained a shred of trust in him, the sound of Paige's voice shattered it to pieces. He'd seen the questions and wariness creep into her beautiful eyes.

For a little longer, he'd have to wear his business hat. Any attempt to clarify would've only pulled at the tenuous threads of their friendship, unraveling what the Lord had begun to weave together. Or had he been doing most of the weaving? Manipulating circumstances to be with Anna every chance he got?

Daniel groaned. Anna must have sensed he was about to kiss her out on the terrace. Her nearness had caused him too easily to slip out of his role of philanthropist. Discretion had taken wing, replaced by a gut-wrenching desire to gather Anna into his arms for one sweet kiss.

But Paige's voice ripped through the space between them like a physical force.

Daniel watched the limo stop at Anna's building. He'd have to press bells at random to gain entrance into her hallway, then pray a New Yorker with his guard down would ring back.

His pulse sped as he watched Nicole and Anna exit the limo. Daniel held his breath, eyeing his firecracker cousin as if he could prevent her from saying something to Anna he'd live to regret.

Nicole hugged Anna, and Daniel exhaled a relieved breath. If Nicole saw him, he was done for. She'd try to find out what he was up to and get a kick out of his undercover efforts.

He sobered as Nicole's whispered message from Jane ran through his mind. Daniel scanned the area for Ted. Apparently, there'd been two phone calls from Ted this morning while Anna showered. One hang-up, and the next a warning message that Anna had better see him today to discuss something urgent. Ted said he'd be "waiting for her."

Daniel's spine snapped straighter. "That's what you think, Ted." To get to Anna, he'd have to go through him first.

Daniel watched the limo pull away then refocused on her building.

Anna entered the interior door. He allowed several seconds to lapse before he hopped out of his car and closed the door.

Hesitating, he reflected on the wisdom of what he was about to do. He had no choice. Who would protect Anna? He pressed a bell and waited. No response. Like a prankster, he pushed several buttons until he finally got a ring back.

He entered the hallway then ascended the stairs two at a time. Moving along the first landing, he tried not to make a sound.

"You rang my bell?" A man's groggy voice asked.

"Sorry," Daniel whispered and continued up the second flight of stairs. The man cursed and slammed the door.

A real gentleman. Daniel shook his head then sat on a step adjacent to Anna's door. If anybody came along, he'd say he was waiting for someone. And he was. Ted. The thug's days of bullying Anna were over.

Staring at Anna's door, Daniel shifted on the step. He could knock and, when she opened the door—before she had time to think or speak—he'd take her in his arms, kiss her, tell her that he loved her.

The *creak* of stairs pulled Daniel out of his musings and to his feet. Holding his breath, he peered over the banister. The top of a head came into view. Brown hair. Denim jacket. *Ted!*

Daniel quickly weighed his options. He could allow Ted to reach Anna's door and have Ted thrown in jail for stalking. But without an order of protection, Ted could claim he stopped by for a friendly visit.

Daniel crept along the hall, reached the head of the staircase, and paused. He looked over the banister again. Nothing. *Show yourself, coward!* He started down the stairs, slowly. Each squeak would tip Ted off to an unwanted presence. A dog barked. Daniel again peered over the railing. Ted's gaze locked on his. In a split second, Ted was running down the stairs.

Daniel sprang into action. Midway down the staircase, he jumped over the railing to the next landing. This time he'd catch the coward. He sped down the next flight and spied the exit door, still partly open. But no Ted.

He arrived outdoors, breathing hard and panning the streets. "Where did he go?"

After a search of the area, Daniel crossed the avenue to his car. He slid down in the front seat, watching the entrance to Anna's building, yet knowing Ted wouldn't have the gall to return tonight.

Daniel gritted his teeth. He shouldn't have kept Ted's antics from Anna. Instead of protecting her, he'd put her in danger. Tomorrow would be a different story. He'd let her know what she was up against—and insist she move out of her apartment.

What if she wouldn't move out? His warning would only serve to frighten her.

With his gaze glued to Anna's building, he decided he would handle this with Ted man-to-man.

ॐ

Giving her e-mail a quick scan, Anna's heart stopped. She opened Aunt Mary's post with a prayer on her lips.

Dearest Anna,

Your enthusiasm is a blessing. When you arrive in Haiti, don't be surprised that everyone knows you. I keep your picture on the bulletin board where all the missionaries can see it, and I brag about you as if you're my own daughter. (Now don't tell your mom I said that.) How are your mom and dad doing? Adam, Lynn, and the boys? And how's your friend, Jane? They're all in my prayers.

As to your question, you're certainly welcome to arrive earlier. I'll be ministering at Precious Children in Africa until December 1. I'd like to be here when you arrive. Can you come after the first of December?

I'm off to my prayer meeting now. When you have a date in mind, let me know. In the meantime, walk in the strength of Jesus. He is the Author and Finisher of your faith. He loves you so much, Anna. In fact, He told me so in my prayers.

My friend, Greta, is calling for me now. So I must stop here.

Love in Jesus,
Aunt Mary

Anna stared at the screen. "Okay, Lord. December it is then."

She snapped off the computer and went to bed without energy enough to remove her clothing.

She held tight to the pillow and released the soft moan of distress that had been stirring in her heart all day. She fought to stay awake so she could pray. But blissful exhaustion overcame her.

Anna closed her eyes and remembered the words of Jesus, which her aunt often used to read aloud from her King James Bible. The verse rang through her heart now. "Peace, be still!"

twenty

Anna scanned Joe Palmer's notes while her crossed leg kept time with her rising panic. She set Joe's wish list on her desk, expelled a breath, and glanced up at the wall clock.

She had twenty minutes to pull herself together before Daniel walked through the door with his parents. Twenty minutes to erase any remnants of her feelings for him and replace them with sound reasoning.

Anna squeezed her eyes shut and recited Philippians 4:13. "I can do everything through him who gives me strength." She opened her eyes and swallowed hard. "I'm doing this for the kids," she whispered.

Now was not the time to fall apart, or she'd disintegrate when she saw him standing in the doorway. She turned in her swivel chair and looked at the door, visualizing Daniel's entrance.

With a shake of her head, she turned back to her desk.

"I can do everything through him who gives me strength."

Anna swiped a stack of reports off her desk, set them on her lap, and began alphabetizing. She stopped to tug at the hem of her straight, navy blue skirt, which kept inching up above her knees.

All she needed was for Daniel to think she'd deliberately changed her style of dress with him in mind. But she had to look professional, and Jane's hand-me-down had saved the day.

Anna stilled her busy fingers. She'd anticipated a lot more flack from Jane after she casually dropped that she'd be leaving for Haiti in December instead of February. After a pause, Jane said, "What about Dan—" And finished with, "Forget it." Jane had finally accepted the futility of her matchmaking efforts. Jane meant well but had a blind spot when it came to Daniel.

Who didn't?

Anna went to the filing cabinet, and plunked the papers into the basket. Dipping her head to scrutinize her clothes, she pressed her hand to her white, button-down blouse. Thanks to Jane, she did look businesslike—if not like a flight attendant.

A soft rap at the door sent her stomach hurtling to her toes. Too early. She wasn't ready for him. Anna took a deep breath. She'd never be ready for him. She crossed the room and pasted on a smile.

She opened the door to find Daniel, front and center, flanked by a man and a woman. He gazed down at her, amusement flickering in his dark eyes. The heat of a blush inched up her face as her eyes shifted from one person to the other and back to Daniel. "Good morning."

"Good morning, Anna." Daniel bowed slightly. He gestured to his right. "This is my father, Antonio."

The mature version of Daniel shook her proffered hand. Anna smiled. "So nice to meet you, Mr. Boccini."

"My pleasure, Anna." He shared Daniel's same voice, but with a heavier Italian accent. "And you call-a me Antonio, please."

Anna nodded, unable to wipe the genuine smile off her face. What a sweet, distinguished gentleman. She'd bet he'd be shocked to know how Daniel had misled her.

"And this is"—Daniel turned slightly—"my mother, Lucia."

Anna shook the woman's delicate hand. With her raven hair pulled back in a chignon at the nape of her neck, she looked the picture of grace and elegance. "Nice to meet you, Mrs. Bo—"

"Lucia." Her greenish eyes lit with a smile.

Anna returned her smile. "Lucia." She stepped back. "Why don't you all come in, please?"

After they filed into the room, she closed the door, stepped to her desk and nearly collapsed into the chair.

With his parents already seated, Daniel sat on the edge of her desk.

Wrapped in a cocoon of his delicious scent, Anna bit her lip and glanced away from him. Her gaze inadvertently came to rest on his mother's face. Hot panic sucked Anna straighter in her chair. Lucia's sympathetic smile. . . She knew!

Anna quickly focused on Antonio. Daniel took the grant envelope from his father, pulled out the papers, and then flipped through them. "Okay, here it is." He leaned forward, so close, the warmth of his breath feathered her face.

"My parents are interested in"—he pointed to the page—"the plans for expansion at this location." Daniel edged the paper toward her so she could get a better look.

Brows drawn, Anna feigned interest, while she waited for her brain to activate.

Daniel cleared his throat. "Anna? Perhaps we can see these premises today?"

She snapped her gaze to his face. *The arrogance of him to be smiling!* "Would you like to see the premises today?" she asked, her chin tilted.

"Yes, that's what I just. . ." Daniel looked at his nodding parents.

"That's fine, of course." Anna swallowed the irritation that she couldn't wait to unleash on Joe Palmer later and forced a smile. "But the premises are on Forty-Seventh Street." She looked at Daniel, half-expecting the prospect of a ten-block jaunt to discourage him enough to want to call it a day.

Daniel's brow furrowed. His father gave her what she'd now come to recognize as a smooth, European shrug. Daniel stroked his chin. "What are you saying, Anna?"

What am I saying? "I–I'm just—"

"Anna's asking"—Lucia leaned forward and looked at her son—"if we'd like to see the premises on Forty-Seventh Street, Daniel." In a gentle voice, Lucia managed to cover the embarrassment Anna felt burning at the tips of her ears.

Lucia definitely knew! *But, thank you, Lucia.*

Anna stood and began gathering her paperwork in haste, avoiding eye contact with Daniel as he spoke to his parents in Italian. Was he making excuses for her insane behavior? *Oh Lord, I'm unraveling. Please do something!*

Antonio and Lucia shuffled out of the room. Anna's heart turned over in her chest. She'd probably ruined any chance of them donating money to The Center.

She stuffed a copy of the grant proposal into her bag. "I'm almost finished. . ."

Daniel didn't move. "Fine, no need to rush."

Raising her lids, her gaze met his. She inhaled deeply, savoring his delicious scent. He had no intention of playing fair.

Anna switched her gaze to her bag, staring into it for all the diversion was worth. "Okay, I think I've got everything." She seized the handles, picked it up, and chanced a glance at him. Only the barest smile shone in his eyes.

Anna gripped the bag handle tighter. Unless she squeezed past him she couldn't move.

Daniel stepped back then waved for her to go ahead of him. "Are you ready?"

"Ready? I think so, I'm—"

"There's no need to be nervous."

Anna looked him in the eye, bristling. "I'm *not* nervous."

Daniel winked. "Good, good, because I'm certain everything will turn out fine."

❧

Daniel hung back observing Anna and his parents interact so naturally they looked like they'd known each other for years. Only when he stood too close did Anna's composure slip. He'd worked hard to gain her trust. Apparently, the phone call from Paige had caused her to resurrect the fortress around her heart. He'd have to come clean with Anna.

"Daniel." His mom's voice echoed off the walls of the drafty room. She waved him over.

He pushed off the wall and joined the three of them around a decayed butcher-block table, making an effort to avoid Anna's gaze. What he needed to confide in her—from his board turning down The Center's original grant request to Paige showing up at his house—would have to wait for later. The exercise in restraint drove him to distraction while he studied the blueprint on the table.

His mom squeezed his arm. "Daniel, Papa and I will discuss this alone later." In Italian, she added they were almost certain they'd donate the building and then she gave Anna her seal of approval. "Sweet and charming," she said with a mother's look that confirmed what he already knew—Anna was a keeper.

Inwardly elated, Daniel nodded but reserved comment. They were *almost* certain they'd approve the grant. Not a yes. He couldn't yet share the information with Anna nor his true feelings for her. Not until he rebuilt her trust in him.

Anna folded the blueprint. "Thank you so much for your time. If you have any other questions just give me a call."

Antonio stepped forward. "You come to our house soon."

"Yes, Anna." Lucia hugged her. "Please visit."

Anna paled, and her smile looked frozen in place. "Oh, thank you."

With a sinking feeling, Daniel watched her fiddle with the papers in her briefcase. She hadn't accepted their invitation. Worse, he sensed she was hiding something.

Daniel filed out of the building behind them. Anna hiding something? He had been the one withholding information from her. His own guilty conscience must be getting the better of him. What could she possibly be hiding? Anna's life was virtually an open book.

twenty-one

Daniel entered Anna's small office and paced around as best as he was able. While he waited for her to finish her meeting with Joe Palmer, he used the time to once again plan how he would articulate all he must convey to her. He anticipated her responses with more than a little dread.

That uneasy feeling he'd been fighting all morning hit him again. Anna had met with him every day for the past two weeks while he toted paperwork as proof they were having meetings—not dates. During that time, she'd spoken often of her passion for helping an orphanage in Haiti. He'd been happy to donate money, but just let him try to switch topics and have a heart-to-heart with her, and Anna would deliberately change the subject. His uneasiness increased. She'd listen to him today.

"Daniel."

He pivoted, smiling without effort. He'd start with the good news first. "Good morning, Anna."

She returned his smile and closed the door. "I hear you have something important to discuss with me?"

"Yes." He pulled out a chair for her. "Have a seat." After she complied, he sat across from her. "My parents—"

Her smile broadened. "Yes?"

"They've decided to donate the building to The Center."

"Oh, wow! Thank you, Lord!" Anna prayed heavenward as she shot to her feet, came around the desk, leaned down, and hugged Daniel. "Thank you."

He placed his hand to the back of her head, cherishing her nearness for as long as she'd allow.

Anna straightened abruptly. She stepped back, as though she'd caught herself off guard, and returned to her seat, her smile still in place. "That is something, isn't it?"

Before he could allow sparks of discouragement to become a raging fire within him, Daniel drew a breath to confess his sins of omission. The most important thing his heart yearned to tell her would have to hold for two more days.

He cleared is throat. "I'd like to discuss a couple of things with you, Anna. First, about that grant. . ."

&

"This one's ready to go." Jane snapped the cap on the black marker.

"Wait." Anna leaned over her. "I need that." She took the marker, knelt beside a carton, and began filling in the return address label. "Do you think you'll still attend Messiah Tabernacle after I'm gone?"

Hearing the dramatic sigh behind her, Anna smiled. Jane enjoyed Pastor Meyers's first sermon enough to return the following Sunday. No doubt the Lord would woo her back again and again.

"I'd love to keep going, but. . ."

Anna recapped the pen and turned. Jane was slumped against the boxes frowning. "The guilt might kill me."

"What?" Anna sat flat on the floor, staring. "Guilt?"

"Yes, guilt." Jane's serious tone got her full attention. "I'd be left to face Daniel in church, and I already feel like a big phony when I'm around him."

Anna drew a sharp breath. "You can't think that way. You've done nothing wrong." She kept her gaze fastened on Jane's face. "It's all *my* fault. I just haven't had a chance to tell him about my plans yet."

"Get serious, Anna." Scowling, Jane sat forward. "You've been out with him almost every night for the past two weeks."

"With good reason!" Looking down at her jeans, Anna picked at the frayed threads. "After the grant stuff was taken care of, we discussed other charities." She shrugged. "And well, I brought up Precious Children, and Daniel wanted to know more, which required more meetings."

"*Meetings?* You keep hiding behind that word so you don't have to face the truth that you're in love with him." Jane stood. "For crying out loud! Last Sunday, I could barely look him in the eye, knowing I was keeping your secret." She took a few abrupt steps to the kitchen table and sank into a chair.

Anna followed. "I'm sorry I put you in this position, okay?" Guilt washed over her. She dropped into the chair adjacent to Jane's.

Jane grunted. "How can you justify it? He's been so honest with you. I can't believe he bothered to explain Paige's phone message to you. I wouldn't have done it if I were in his shoes." She sighed. "That had to be embarrassing for him."

"You're right. I have to tell him, even as a friend. I've tried, but the right moment never seemed to come. It's complicated."

"Not really." Jane sank back against the chair. "You're afraid he can persuade you to stay in New York. And if you stay, you're afraid of a repeat performance of what happened with Ted. Am I right?"

The stinging accusation hit full force. Whatever she felt for Daniel terrified her. She had no frame of reference. Certainly not Ted. She shot Jane a tight smile. "See all those boxes?" Anna pointed toward the other room. "Do I look like I'm about to change my mind?"

"Fine." Jane slammed the table. "Then tell him the truth already!"

Anna dropped her gaze to the placemat and began smoothing out the wrinkles. "Daniel and I are not alike at all. We have different values." She looked Jane straight in the eye, feeling the strength of her convictions to her toes. "With his lifestyle, all that money, I could never feel comfortable—"

"Ha!" Jane bristled. "You were comfortable enough—overjoyed, in fact—when Daniel and his family donated the building to The Center. Isn't that as significant to God as missionary work?"

"Of course it is. And you're right." A burst of nervous energy brought her to her feet. "I need to tell him I'm leaving." Anna nodded. She could do it. Daniel would be happy for her.

"I promise I'll tell him tomorrow."

"Um, it wouldn't be right to tell him over the phone." Jane sighed. "And tomorrow you're coming out to Queens to meet me for dinner, remember?"

Anna scanned the room. With so much on her to-do list, how could she afford the leisure time? But she'd promised. "Yes, I'll be there."

"Are you taking the train in?"

"No. I told Daniel I was going into Queens to meet you, and well, you know Daniel. . ." Her face warmed. "He said it was too dangerous to travel by train at night." She shrugged. "He's sending Nicole to pick me up."

"Hmm." Jane grinned. "Traveling in style again?"

"I guess." She tried to smile, but her face grew taut. "Please tell me you won't let my behavior stop you from attending church."

Jane waved her away. "Oh, don't start feeling guilty." She heaved a sigh. "I'll go back, okay?"

Anna smiled. "And I promise, I'll tell Daniel, Sunday. . .before service even, that I'm leaving for Haiti."

Instead of getting the look of satisfaction she expected, Jane glanced up at her as if she were about to cry.

Anna turned and went back into the middle room. She had a feeling digging deeper would unearth more than she could handle tonight.

twenty-two

Anna stepped outside her building, opened her umbrella, and looked across the avenue.

Nicole waved from the car window.

Anna lifted her hand in acknowledgment then danced around puddles to the corner.

As she waited for the light to change, Anna held tight to the umbrella, which flapped like a wind sail. She glanced over her shoulder at her building. There was still so much left to do. If only she hadn't promised Jane they'd have dinner together.

Checking for traffic, her gaze moved from the fast-approaching taxi to the swamp at her feet. Anna jumped back, gasping as the spray of cold water drenched her stockings. *"Get gussied up!"* Why had she listened to Jane? She darted across the street in pursuit of the warmth of the car.

"*Ciao*, Anna." A smiling Nicole looked up from the open car window. "You sit in front with me?"

"Definitely." Anna scooted around the tail of the car, her shoes sucking up water as she ran to the passenger door and opened it.

"I help you?"

"No thanks, Nicole, I'm fine." Struggling with her umbrella, she finally snapped it shut, and jumped into the front seat. She pulled the door closed and sighed. "Oh, this weather!"

"*Sì, e freddo.*" Nicole motioned with a mock shiver. "You tell me how to go to restaurant, okay?"

Anna smiled. "Sure. Straight ahead, for now." Settling back, she positioned her cold legs close to the vent blowing warm air. *Gussied up.* She should've worn her cozy khakis and a sweater. She unbuttoned her coat, slid her hand under it to her ribs, and pulled at the stretchy material of her black dress.

116

"Anna?" Nicole tapped the dashboard. "I play *musica*?"

"Oh, wait, make a left here. . ." Anna gestured. "Sorry. . .yes, *musica* is fine."

Nicole made a sweeping turn to get onto the bridge.

Anna grabbed the seat-belt buckle and fastened herself in, then glanced at Nicole. With a new sense of dread, she watched her flip through a CD album on the seat beside her. Anna held her breath, feeling the car slide over the wet grids of the Fifty-ninth Street bridge, eyeing the river below. "Do you need help?"

Nicole held up a CD. "I find it." She popped the disc into the player.

Anna exhaled then looked out her window and swept her gaze over the sparkling Manhattan skyline. Lights, like a million stars, winked from skyscrapers. The Empire State Building stood above it all, its steeple donned in red, white, and blue. Italian music wafted to her ears.

She took a deep breath, feeling her snug dress pinch her awake. This was no time to fall in love with New York City. No time to fall in love.

"You like Andrea Bocelli?" Nicole asked.

Another Italian relative? Anna turned. "Who?"

"The singer." She pointed to the dashboard. "Bocelli? You like him?"

"Oh, I never heard him before." She grinned at Nicole's perky enthusiasm. "Beautiful music though."

"You don't know Andrea?" Her olive eyes widened.

Anna shook her head. She had rarely listened to music or just plain relaxed. Not until she met Daniel, and then, the scales tipped too far in the opposite direction.

"What's he singing?"

Nicole smiled. "Ah, this song is 'Cantico.' Andrea, he is singing. . ." She tilted her head, moving to its rhythm. " 'Why are you crying? Don't think! Just hold me.' "

Don't think? Anna nodded slowly. Sweet sentiments for a song. But the feeling of impending doom in the pit of her stomach had everything to do with not thinking.

"And now, Andrea says, 'I never give up trying,' " Nicole continued with impassioned determination. " 'Don't run away from me, you are mine.' " She gave a toss of her head, sending her dark hair flying around her face. "Ah, I love-a love."

Anna sighed. Romantic songs and rain—the combination would make anybody ache for their one true love. She sat up straighter. But blind love had a way of sneaking up on the unsuspecting with gentle hands. And then what?

"Daniel loves you, huh?"

Anna's breath caught. Nicole wriggled her shoulders in an enthused little dance.

"*Daniel loves. . .*" Anna shook her head. "I don't know, I. . ." Only one person could've planted such a notion in Nicole's head. Jane!

Nicole frowned. "You don't know?" She made a clucking sound. "And you? You love Daniel, too?"

Too? No-boundaries, out-of-control Jane had done a thorough job of it. Anna's throat constricted. "I—we're good friends." She stared straight ahead. "You need to make a right when you get off this exit."

She clasped her shaking hands. Her heart pounded harder. "A left at this corner, Nicole." Anna's fingers curled into fists. She pushed forward in the seat, willing the car to move faster toward Jay-Jay's, to the moment when she could chat with her so-called friend.

"Right here."

Nicole swung into the lot, parked, and snapped off the headlights.

Anna unfastened her seat belt, her fingers trembling. "It's okay, Nicole, you don't have to wait for me."

"Okay." Nicole nodded, clicked off the ignition, and pulled out the key.

Anna measured her breaths before speaking. "Thank you, Nicole, but you can go now."

"I walk you in," she said smiling.

Anna blew out a breath, got out of the car, and closed the door. At least the rain had let up. She took long strides over the gravel lot to the front door.

Nicole opened the wooden door, sending restaurant noises pouring into the silent street.

Anna stepped inside and turned to say good-bye, but Nicole happily followed her in.

Daniel must have anticipated the Saturday night crowd and asked Nicole to see her to the table. The heat of a blush came over her, quickly dampened by a rising indignity as she scanned the tables in search of her chatty friend.

Nicole tapped her shoulder. "Maybe in the back?"

Anna nodded, then squeezed through the obstacle course of patrons, wait staff, and tables. The back of the restaurant? She turned with the question on her lips, but Nicole slipped in front of her, sped up a few steps, and pushed open the swinging door.

Anna's eyes widened. "There *is* a back!"

Nicole smiled. "Dancing." She pointed to the wooden rectangle in the corner.

A smile tugged at Anna's lips as she watched couples moving in a slow dance. She took a deep breath and looked away. "Let's find Jane." Her gaze skittered over the tables in the semicircle room.

"Maybe over there?" Nicole gestured to an area around the curve of the wall. Anna shrugged and followed Nicole around the bend.

Anna stopped dead in her tracks, her gaze fastened on Daniel. All at once, joy and panic fueled her shaky legs, pushing her forward. Her gaze went to the other faces. . .the balloons tied to the chairs.

"Surprise!"

❧

Daniel stood. He tapped his jacket pocket to check for the gift box. Reaching out, he clasped Anna's hand and squeezed it. "Happy birthday, Anna." He leaned down and touched his lips to the coolness of her cheek.

"I—I. . .thank you."

Jane inched around the table, embraced Anna, and screeched, "Happy birthday!"

Anna greeted Lucia and Jane's mom, Eleanor, then came full circle. Smiling, she looked at Nicole. "Thank you."

Nicole hugged her then applauded. "I did good, Daniel, huh?"

"You did great, Nicole." Daniel tapped his hand to his pocket again. Everything in him wanted to give Anna the ring now. He helped her out of her coat. He'd have to wait till they were alone. After dinner.

Daniel's heart picked up speed at the sight of her in the black dress. "Anna, you look fantastic." He pulled out a chair for her then sat down.

"Thank you." The pink hint of a blush highlighted her cheekbones. She looked away from him quickly. "Thank you, everyone, for being here. I've never had a surprise birthday party."

"Jane's idea," Daniel said.

Anna jabbed his arm with her elbow. "And how long have *you* known?"

Jane waved. "I told Daniel and Nicole about the party about two weeks ago." She laughed.

"Leave it to you, Jane." Anna's face lit with a smile. "And Eleanor, I'm so glad to see you. It's been months."

"Too long." Eleanor, blue-eyed, blond, and as sassy as Jane, shook her head. "I'm sitting here speechless, Anna. Wow, have you changed."

"Have I?" Anna ran her hand down her hair.

"Your hair is the same." Eleanor laughed. "But Daniel's right, you look fantastic-o."

"Well, thank you."

Nicole clapped, garnering everybody's attention. "Maybe Anna, she's in love?"

Daniel smiled amidst the laughter and gave Anna a sidelong glance. Their eyes locked. Anna looked away quickly. "Thank you for coming, Lucia."

"I *had* to be here for such a big night." Lucia smiled. "Antonio would've come, too, but he's away on business."

"I understand, of course." Anna leaned sideways to give the busboy leeway as he filled her water glass. Daniel clasped his hand around Anna's bare upper arm and pulled her closer. "Are you really surprised?"

He felt a rush of relief at the sound of her laughter. "Yes!"

"What? What's funny?" Nicole asked.

"Nothing." Daniel patted Anna's head, pushing away his niggling doubts. The surprise of the party made the nervousness he sensed in her understandable. Before the night's end, his prayers would be answered.

A waiter approached the table. "Are you ready to order now?"

Daniel dragged his attention away from Anna and nodded.

❧

What would they all think of her after she broke the news? Anna forced down the last bite of her meal. What did Jane mean by putting her in this awkward predicament?

The ice rattled in the glass as she brought the tea to her lips. Jane was not to blame. The agony ripping through her soul had everything to do with being too afraid of her feelings to be truthful with Daniel.

"Anna?" Daniel stood, reached his hand out to her. "Walk with me."

She stared up at him, held still by the emotion in his eyes. He scooped her hand in his, and the slightest tug brought her to her feet and out of her chair.

He led her away from the table, around the bend, closer to the sound of Nat King Cole singing "Unforgettable."

Daniel drew her into the circle of his arms. She had allowed herself to dream of how it might feel to be in his arms, but nothing had prepared her for the rough tickle of his cheek against hers, the feel of his heart beating in time with her own. Anna closed her eyes.

Daniel hummed the melody, his lips brushing her face. He drew back slightly, and she looked up into his eyes. "*Ti amo*, Anna."

A tremor ran through her. Her face grew hot as her eyes filled.

He pressed his lips to her forehead. Looking down into her face again, his dark eyes spoke the words before he repeated in English, "I love you, Anna." He placed his hand to the back of her head and drew her against his shoulder.

She was trembling now. What had she done!

"Anna Banana! Is that you?"

Daniel swung around.

Anna's jaw dropped open. A gasp of horror stuck in her throat as her eyes refused to believe Ted stood in front of her.

twenty-three

Ted placed his hand over his heart. "I hear you're leaving, Anna." He thrust his other hand toward her. "I stopped in to say good-bye."

Daniel edged his way between them. "You said good-bye to Anna weeks ago. I think you'd better leave."

Ted backed up hastily, hands lifted in a motion of surrender.

Daniel stepped forward. "And don't come around Anna again. I've had enough of you." The calm in Daniel's voice, the blaze of his dark eyes, froze Anna's feet to the floor.

"Daniel, please." Her words came out a hoarse whisper from her taut, dry throat.

"It's all right, Anna." Daniel spoke without taking his eyes off Ted. "Go back to the table."

Ted took another step back. "Whoa, I'm not looking for any trouble."

The sights and sounds of the room melted away. Anna gripped the wooden rail bordering the dance floor. Daniel's hands tightened into fists.

"Not looking for trouble?" Daniel pointed in her direction. "Why are you following Anna?"

Ted's mouth opened in a pathetic show of surprise. "Okay, I get it. You think I followed her?"

Daniel slipped his hands into his pockets. "I *know* you followed her, and I'm giving you two seconds to get out of here." He flicked a brief glance her way. Anna gripped the rail tighter. "My Christian witness and not upsetting Anna are the only reasons you're still standing. Now leave."

"No problem." Ted shook his head as though Daniel had misconstrued his intentions. He shot a glance her way, a mock smile lifting one corner of his mouth. "Good luck in Haiti,

Anna. You always wanted out of New York—" His departing footfalls landed like a drumbeat on her ears.

Daniel pivoted, his dark eyes regarding her. "Haiti? What's he up to now, saying you're leaving New York?" The grin he wore revealed he didn't believe Ted.

Anna heard nothing but the sound of her blood roaring in her ears, saw nothing but Daniel's face, his grin fading, dawning in his eyes, and then the muscle in his jaw tighten as truth dawned.

Anna reached for his arm. "I–I'm sorry. I should have told you, Daniel. I'm so sorry."

❧

Anna kept her eyes downcast. "What did you tell Jane and the others?"

Daniel switched his gaze to the floor of the limo. He had no intention of feeling sorry for her, though she looked lost sitting alone on the big bench seat at the rear of the limo.

"I drove my mother to the restaurant." What a blind fool he'd been. "She'll drive my car back to the city." He had tried to appear composed when he broke the news that he and Anna had to leave. Jane didn't look at him, and her mother Eleanor seemed baffled. "No birthday cake?" Eleanor's question was met with a warning glare from Jane. Apparently, Jane had known all along of Anna's plans—as did Ted!

Daniel released a pent-up breath. "I told Jane and her mother good night for you. I told them Nicole was driving us back to your place."

Anna's head snapped up. "Do they know Ted was in the restaurant?"

"Ted!" Daniel grunted. He had held back telling Anna he loved her to give her time to trust him. And this is how his patience was rewarded. "They didn't see *Ted*." He struck his fisted hand against his thigh. "Why didn't you tell me the truth, Anna?"

Staring out the side window, she shook her head. "I don't know."

That much he did believe. "I suppose you had no idea I

was falling in love with you?" He fell back against the seat, feeling defeated to the core. "That I loved you from the moment I saw you?"

Anna blinked quickly. "Why talk about it? I'm leaving."

How misguided could she be? Daniel scrubbed his hand across his jaw. "So I've heard." If she had taken a knife and run it through his heart, the ragged pain in his chest could be no greater. "You know, now that I'm thinking back, you had so many opportunities to let me know you were planning to leave. We—"

"I told you—" Anna closed her eyes. "I'm sorry."

Sorry? Daniel gave a mild snort of a laugh. "*Sorry* is when you bump into a stranger on the street. We discussed the orphanage. All along, you knew." He unbuttoned his coat and loosened his tie, as if he could free his growing agitation. "Obviously, I meant nothing to you."

"Don't say that, Daniel." She pinned him with a tearful gaze. "Don't ask anymore questions. Please."

"All right." There was no point to it. "I won't ask you anything—anymore." How long would it take to push her out of his mind? Out of his heart? The thought of starting over with someone else—impossible.

Anna backhanded a tear from her cheek. "You don't understand."

"No, I don't understand!" Had he imagined all of it? The torment drove him forward to sit beside her. "Anna?"

Her tearful gaze snapped to meet his. He had to know if she loved him. If she refused to answer with words. . .

Daniel cupped her face with his hands. He rubbed away the remnant of her tears with his thumbs.

&

Anna leaned closer. He was like a magnet pulling her to him. His kisses burned a trail down her face to her lips. Clutching the lapels of his coat, she sank into his embrace. Her eyes closed against the unbearable tenderness of his kiss.

No! She unclenched her fingers and pushed against his solid chest. "No. . ."

Daniel drew back, turned away, and plowed his fingers through his hair. He stared straight ahead. "You won't let me love you, will you?" Resting his elbows on his knees, he gazed down at the floor. "You don't trust me. Is that it?"

Anna squeezed her eyes shut, fighting the temptation to fall back into the safety of his strong arms. She listened to his breathing, tasted the remnant of his kiss on her lips.

Daniel turned his gaze on her. "Tell me, have I done something to hurt you?"

She shook her head. She had tried hard to find reasons to accuse him. A painless way to say good-bye. Anna swallowed past the ache in her throat. "No. We're just. . .different."

His humorless laugh echoed through the car. "Different?" He spat out the word. "You're driving me crazy, Anna."

The memory of the warmth of his kiss washed over her. She forced her gaze away from him and pulled her coat tighter around her waist.

Daniel clamped his hand on her wrist. "If I gave up my worldly possessions, would that make you happy?"

She answered the hypothetical quesion with a shake of her head. Even if he was serious, he'd eventually resent her for depriving him of the only lifestyle he'd ever known. "I'd never ask you to do that." She hadn't intended to fall in love. She never planned this. "The Lord put the burden for these children on my heart. I'll be living in one of the poorest countries on earth." She swiped at another tear. Daniel reached into his pocket, pulled out a hankie, and handed it to her.

"Thank you." Anna pressed the silk cloth to her face, inhaling his scent, already missing him. "You know enough about the orphanage by now. No food, no medicines, no bathrooms. Children roam the streets starving. And you live like—"

"A king?" He turned to her swiftly. "I can send money, Anna." He grasped her hand, and she held on tight. "It's not as if I don't understand. My heart has been touched by the children, as well."

"It's more than that."

Daniel brushed back her hair with his fingers. "Don't cry, okay?" He gathered her into his arms. She could stay in his arms forever, she knew. She could take the easy way out. "Don't cry," he whispered, stroking the back of her head, rocking her. "Maybe this is what happens when idealistic and materialistic crash head-on, huh?"

Her heart crushed under the weight of his kindness. She drew back and looked into his eyes. "I'll be gone for two years, and then. . ."

Daniel nodded. "We never know what the Lord has in store." The sadness in his eyes told her another story.

The car stopped in front of her building. Daniel got out and opened her door. "I'm pretty resourceful, Anna. And I can win my way through most things. But no matter how I try, I can't seem to scale that wall you've built around your heart."

He leaned down and touched his lips to hers in a brief kiss. "Good-bye, Anna, I'll be praying for you."

"Yes." She could change her mind. But she'd be the same weakling she'd been with Ted. "I'll pray for you, too."

"Thank you." He straightened and held the door wide open. "You have my number. If you need anything. . . Well, you know."

Anna nodded quickly, slipping past him, out of his life. Isn't this what she had prayed for since the first day she met him? And now the Lord had removed the temptation forever.

Anna pushed the key into the lock of the foyer door. The thud of the limo door reached her ears. Pain wrapped around her heart, squeezing the last drop of hope from her. *Don't go, Daniel. Please don't go! Lord, Lord, I'm begging you to do something!*

Hot tears slipped down her cheeks. She'd never been so torn. A part of her felt relief. It was over. She was free to go to Haiti. Another part wanted to turn and run straight back into Daniel's arms.

She pushed open the door, walked straight ahead, and trod up the stairs, lost in a slow-motion nightmare. Numbly, she passed her neighbors' doors.

She started up the second flight, stopped, and looked up.

The dead bulb on the next landing plunged the remaining steps and the second floor into darkness. A chill scuttled up her spine.

Anna tightened her grip on the wooden banister, drew a shaky breath, and continued forward. Ted had already done his damage tonight at Jay-Jay's. He wouldn't be back.

Neither would Daniel.

The thought brought fresh tears surging to her eyes. She blinked them away, pressed the palm of her hand to the wall, and felt her way through the darkness. A sense of doom breathed down her neck. She bit back panic, stepping lightly down the hall.

She reached her front door and fumbled with the jangling key ring.

Click. A shadow jumped to the wall. Her heart jolted; a soft gasp escaped her.

"You can see now, can you?"

Anna spun, her heart thudding in her throat. "Mrs. O'Leary!" She slumped against the wall, fighting for breath.

The old woman kept her door chained, eyeing her through the thin vertical line of space. " 'Tis dangerous."

"Oh—yes, I have to find my key." Anna held fast to her key chain, her hands shaking. "Just a second." She scrambled through them.

"I've got it." She slipped the key into the lock, twisted, and shoved her door open. "Thank—"

The woman's door snapped shut. Anna dove inside her kitchen, closed, and locked the door, then glanced over her shoulder.

Glued to the spot, she stared at the refrigerator, at the magnet that should be holding the paper with her flight information. Her gaze shot to the counter. She caught her breath. A fit of trembling seized her. Ted had been here. That's how he knew about Haiti. "Lord, give me peace."

Anna moved to the table, unable to feel the floor beneath her feet. She lifted her gaze to the rooms beyond her kitchen, pressed her cold fingers to her lips, and stared into the darkness of her bedroom. A hot tremor started in the pit of her stomach, spreading over her skin. Traffic noises wafted to her ears. Ted. Had he gone into her bedroom, too?

She fought back a surge of nausea and reached her hand around the wall, feeling for the light switch wedged behind the stacked cartons. With her eyes trained ahead, she flicked the switch. *Light!* A breath whooshed out of her. The dim glimmer of the lamp buried behind more boxes gave her momentary respite.

A sound, a light shuffle, grabbed her attention. She jerked toward the front door. "Who's there?" Her voice cracked. *Nothing. Nothing.* Her imagination.

She stepped over a carton, edged her way toward her bedroom, and stopped abruptly in the doorway.

The thudding of her heart competed with the sound of wind thrashing through the window. Had she opened the window? *No...maybe!*

The gauzy curtains danced a crazy, twisted rhythm in time with the gust of wind sweeping across the floor.

Anna hugged her own arms to herself. Her mouth went dry. She set one foot into her bedroom, the other poised for flight. She reached in and toggled the light switch.

"Ted!"

Ted's heavy hand clamped Anna's wrist. He yanked her toward him. A scream ripped from her throat.

Ted swore and pressed his other hand over her mouth, his fingers cutting into her lips. The taste of blood touched her tongue.

Anna reached behind, writhing, punching wildly with her free hand. He dragged her backwards. She poised her fingers to claw, raked them down his cheek, and then closed her hand tight around a clump of hair.

❧

Daniel continued sitting in the double-parked limo, window open, the feel of bitter wind on his face a welcome distraction.

But there was no sense waiting. Anna wouldn't reemerge with a change of heart. "We can go now, Nicole."

As she started into traffic, Daniel looked up at Anna's window.

"Stop the car!" Daniel leaped from the still-moving limo and raced toward Anna's building. He heard Anna's scream! He knew it was Anna! *Please, Lord, please! Get me into that building.*

"What's wrong?" Nicole's panicked voice shot from the car window.

Daniel spun. "Call 9-1-1. . .apartment 2-E." He dove into the foyer, tore off his suit jacket, and wrapped it around his fisted hand. He punched through the glass pane and turned the knob. He pulled back his arm. A jagged shard of glass sliced his flesh.

He pushed open the door and flew up the steps, racing past a shouting tenant. At the next flight he slammed into a wall of darkness and loped forward haphazardly. He pressed his left hand over his arm to stop the flow of blood seeping through his shirt.

Plunging across the landing, he ran his hands over Anna's door to the knob and turned it. Locked! He bashed his shoulder against the door, drew back, and bashed it again. The sound of splintering wood echoed through the hall. The force propelled him back against her neighbor's door.

He positioned his hands against the doorjamb and kicked with the force of fury rising in him.

Anna screamed. The sound crashed against his eardrums. Daniel catapulted forward. The door slapped open, clattering against the wall as he skidded to a stop in her apartment. He turned, scanning the room, then rushed forward as he spotted Anna, sprawled atop boxes, blood on her face. Ted stood over her, staring toward the shattered door.

"Don't touch her!"

"You!" Ted cursed and stumbled backward over a carton.

Daniel leaped forward, clamping a viselike grip on his jacket collar. "You're not going anywhere, you coward!" He yanked him into the kitchen. Ted flailed his arms and swung his fist at Daniel's jaw. Daniel's head snapped back.

"Daniel!"

Anna's scream rang in his ears. Daniel drew back his hand and launched a blow that took Ted with a solid, satisfying crack on his jaw.

Ted crashed against the wall, blinked, and then slid into a heap on the floor.

Breathing hard, his hands still fisted, Daniel stood over him. Ted didn't move. Daniel shifted his gaze to Anna, huddled in a corner, fingers pressed to her bloodied lip. "Are you all right?"

Anna's frightened gaze stayed glued to his face. She nodded. "Your arm. Oh, Daniel, your arm!"

"It's all right. Get up." Daniel offered his hand. Hers was trembling. He pulled her forward. The sounds of sirens screamed up to her apartment from the open windows.

Daniel stared at Ted, out cold on the floor. "Here lies the man you've judged me by!" He jammed his hand into his pocket, pulled out all his cash, and threw it on her table. "This will pay for the damage to the door downstairs. And this. . ." He gestured to her broken locks and moved toward the dark hall. "I'll give my statement to the police downstairs."

"Daniel, wait. Let me bandage your—"

"What? What, Anna?" His eyes burned down to hers. "There is no bandage for my wound. The police are on their way. You'll be all right now. Good-bye, Anna."

twenty-four

"My brother Adam called. He'll be taking my apartment." Anna folded another summer dress and placed it in her suitcase.

"That's great." Jane smiled. "Do you want these?" She held a pair of ragged blue shorts in her hand.

"No, you can put them in the throwaway pile."

"So Adam will take over your lease? That'll get you off the hook for the rent." Jane sat on the edge of the bed. "And you won't have to ship this bed back to Akron."

"Yeah, that would've cost a pretty penny." Anna zipped her suitcase closed. "Can you do me a favor?"

Jane got to her feet. "Sure. What?"

"Oh, I don't mean right now." She picked up an empty suitcase and set it atop the bed. "When Adam comes, can you help him organize? He's a great guy, but he's kind of helter-skelter." Anna looked around the room. "You know what stuff I want mailed to Akron. I'll leave you the money."

"You got it. But you don't have to leave money." Jane rummaged through the pile of clothing. "Daniel said, 'Whatever Anna needs. . .'" She cleared her throat. "Anyway, he didn't only mean he'd sponsor your trip, he said, 'Any costs associated with it.'"

Anna flipped open the bag, studiously avoiding Jane's eyes. "In case I do come back to New York, I won't have to worry about Ted anymore. To think he was roaming around my apartment, going through my things. And if it hadn't been for Daniel. . ." She shivered, refusing to relive the incident.

Jane stood beside her, folding a blouse. "I wouldn't trust Ted even with the order of protection. What a maniac!"

Anna waved. "Yeah, well, good riddance."

"And it could've been worse. Good thing Daniel was looking out for you." Jane dropped the blouse into the suitcase. "He actually stayed in the hallway, guarding your door a couple of nights."

The clothes in Anna's hands slipped through her fingers, tumbling to the floor. "No, he didn't."

"Okay." Jane shrugged. "Are you taking this?"

Anna ignored the item dangling from her fingers. "What makes you say such things?"

Jane grinned. "Your neighbor, remember? The guy sleeping beside your door?" She snorted. "That wasn't Ted, sweetie."

Anna slammed the lid of the suitcase, turned, and headed toward the kitchen.

"What? What did I say?" Jane's voice trailed from behind her.

Anna opened the refrigerator door then slammed it closed. "I don't know why you bothered to tell me that now."

Jane shrugged. "I guess I—"

"You know what. . ." Anna pushed back her hair from her face. "I don't want an answer. Let's just drop it."

"Sorry." Jane turned. "I'll go get the packed bag."

"Wait." Anna took a breath. "I'm sorry, too. I really am. Tomorrow's the big day. I guess my nerves are frayed."

Jane nodded. "That's understandable. If it were me, I'd. . ." She pivoted and walked toward the bedroom.

Anna stared after her. Why were they all being so reasonable? She didn't deserve it, especially not from Daniel. He was actually sending Nicole to drive her to the airport—or so she'd discovered through the third-party message from Jane.

Dropping into a kitchen chair, Anna eyed the calendar on the refrigerator. A little over two weeks had passed since her disastrous twenty-fifth birthday party. More than two weeks since she'd seen Daniel or spoken with him. She closed her eyes, forcing his name out of her head.

Jane padded into the kitchen, suitcase in hand. She set it down next to the door. "Sorry I won't be able to see you off tomorrow."

"No, don't be." Anna managed a smile. "You have clients. You have to work."

"Yeah, but. . ." Jane shrugged. "You know, the only good thing Ted ever did was to bring you to Manhattan. You have no idea how much I'm going to miss you."

Anna's throat tightened. She stood. "I'll miss you, too." She opened the refrigerator door. "Want something to drink?"

"No thanks." Jane sat. "Boy, your brother is going to love these flowery chairs."

Anna laughed while pouring the iced tea. "I never thought of that, but it's funny." She ran her gaze over the chairs. "I'm trying to picture six-foot-two Adam McCort sitting here. Too much."

"Listen." Jane stood. "I'm sorry I was pushy when it came to Daniel." She wore a sad smile. "It's only that I believed you two were made for one another."

Anna's heart plummeted. She shook her head and set her empty glass in the sink. "No. We weren't 'made for one another.'" Her own words bit her soul. "I know you meant well though." She looked away from Jane. "I'd better finish packing."

❧

Nicole stood on the curb at JFK airport, rubbing her mitten-clad hands together, her dark eyes tear filled.

Anna tried to smile but tears rose in her eyes. "Thank you for driving me."

Nicole nodded. "God bless you, Anna."

A pang of guilt stabbed her heart. Matchmaker or not, Nicole had never been a nuisance. And now, saying their final good-byes, she realized they'd formed a sisterly bond. Anna clutched the collar of her coat, determined not to yield to more tears. "God bless you, too."

Nicole smiled. "I miss you, and Daniel will, he. . ." Her brows drew together. She rushed forward, and they fell into a mutual embrace. Nicole kissed her cheek, patted her head, and stepped back. "*Ciao*, Anna." With her eyes downcast, she turned, and walked around the car.

Good-bye, Nicole. Anna swallowed the ache in her throat and hefted the suitcases from the sidewalk. She walked slowly into the terminal, took her place at the end of a long line, and dropped the luggage at her feet.

She scanned the terminal, trying to steady her short, shaky breaths. Why lie to herself? She'd hoped for a last-minute phone call from Daniel and, more foolishly, a personal appearance.

Anna pushed her bags with the toe of her shoe, inching forward in line. Only a reckless dreamer would expect Daniel to show up, give her a secret smile, as though she hadn't destroyed his trust and love for her.

Still...

Anna glanced over her shoulder, surveying the area for a sign of him. The tension she'd felt in church as she waited for a glimpse of Daniel, tightened in her stomach now.

She faced forward, squaring her shoulders. Since the surprise party, Jane told her, Daniel had been attending the evening services. Of course, he'd want to avoid her. Anna shuffled forward in line, tears balancing on her lower lids.

There was no chance for reconciliation. Because she'd hidden the truth from him, even the hope of a friendship was impossible.

Anna arrived at the counter, hefted her suitcases onto the scale, then handed her passport to the man behind the desk.

"Any seating preference?" he asked, twitching his mustache.

"No, it doesn't matter." Anna peeked over her shoulder again. Why look for him anyway? She'd pushed Daniel out of her way to get where she was going. She turned back to the clerk, watching him punch keys, hastening her to her destination.

He slipped tags through the handles of her bags then glanced up. "You're all set." He handed back her passport and the ticket. "Gate 16. First stop Miami. Have a nice flight."

"Thank you." Anna picked up her carry-on and walked toward the gate slowly. She stopped in front of the escalator and turned one last time. There'd be no more surprise visits from Daniel.

Anna stepped onto the moving staircase. This is what she wanted. And if second thoughts teased her sensibilities, she must do what God expected of her.

≥å

Daniel dragged his hand over his snow-damp hair. He sat forward in the cab and knocked on the divider. "Can you go faster?"

The longhaired driver ceased jerking his head to the noise that he apparently considered music and glanced back. "I'm trying." He resumed bobbing his head. "Bad weather."

"Bad weather." Daniel scanned the lanes of bumper-to-bumper traffic on the Grand Central Parkway. Why had he let Anna go without saying good-bye? He should've gone to the morning church service. Made small talk.

Would it have changed anything?

A truck roared onto the entrance ramp, bringing two lanes of stalled cars to a complete stop.

What kind of man would let Anna leave this way? He had declared his love one minute, avoided her like the plague the next.

He tugged at the knot in his tie. She'd given him an opening when she said she'd be gone for two years. After that? Maybe time would've changed something. She might've come to realize she could trust him. But on the very night he believed with his whole heart he would slip an engagement ring on Anna's finger, hope failed him, and he had virtually said good-bye forever.

Daniel stared out the window and sent up a silent plea. *Please, Father, make a way. Let me see Anna one last time. Just one last time.*

He glanced at his watch. In less than half an hour he wouldn't have a chance to make it up to her.

He rested against the seat and closed his eyes. The whine of car horns and screaming electric guitars blasting from the radio speakers filled his head. He would make no attempt to persuade Anna to stay in New York. She believed God called her to Haiti. Why couldn't he believe it? Or did he want his will instead of God's?

Feeling the car bump along faster, Daniel opened his eyes. It would be a miracle if he made it in time to see her off. Maybe the Lord would come through at the eleventh hour.

He sat forward and caught sight of a green overhead sign indicating the entrance to JFK. "I want the American departures terminal. Okay?"

The cabbie jabbed the air with his fisted hand, Daniel counted out money for the fare, his mind racing. What would he say to her?

The car curved around one dizzying circle then rounded another. Whoever designed the airport must have been listening to the same music as the cabbie.

The cab stopped. Daniel stashed money into the metal tray. Before the cab pulled to the curb, he jumped out and closed the door.

With his heart drumming, he strode through the automatic doors into the American terminal. He went to the bank of monitors that listed flights. Scanning each screen, he saw it. *Gate 16.* He moved with long, determined strides to the escalator. He knew security wouldn't permit him past the gates. If Anna had gone past that point, he'd never see her again.

He took the stairs two at a time, squeezed past a man with a briefcase, then headed toward the security booths. He stopped, taking time for a breath, while he surveyed the long lines.

He gazed past the X-ray machines, at the end of the conveyor belt. . .

Could it be?

The petite blond turned, and his heart sank. He was too late. He clamped his jaw tight, scanned the rows of passengers again, and turned away.

Good-bye, Anna. I love you.

twenty-five

A scream emerged from the pit of Anna's stomach, piercing her own ears. She burst out of the bathroom, jerking up her pajama bottoms, stumbling blindly toward her room.

"Oh, dear!" Her aunt called from the darkness of the bedroom. "What did you see now?" The light flicked on.

Anna huddled in the middle of her bed, gasping, her fingers tangled in her hair.

Mary stood over her, shaking her gray head. "The bathroom again?"

"Some—" Anna nodded. "Big thing."

Mary sat beside her and patted her head. "You've managed to find more creatures in the bathroom in a couple of weeks than I've encountered in all my years."

Anna fought for breaths. "I feel like. . .they're after me." She looked at her aunt's smiling, creamy-skinned face. If only Aunt Mary's peace were contagious.

"I'll go check." Mary rose. "But it's probably only Ben."

"No." Anna squeezed her trembling hands together. "It wasn't a person, it was—"

"A rat." Mary took off in the direction of the bathroom next door to the bedroom they shared in back of the orphanage.

"Lord," Anna whispered, "please, please help me!" Goose-bumps inched up her arms, spreading quickly over her entire body. She heard her aunt's footsteps and gathered a calming breath.

"Yep." Mary stood over her, hands on her slim hips. "Judging by the trail, Ben paid us a little visit." She sat on the side of the single bed. "Forget Ben. You're a bag of bones, my darling niece. I know the food here isn't what you're used to, but—"

"The food's fine." Anna tucked her trembling hands under

her thighs. She could hack this.

"Then it's something else." Mary stood, crossed to her own bed, and sat facing her.

"I wish"—Anna sucked in a breath—"I could be you."

"Well, now!" Mary sighed. "Wouldn't that be a hoot? Two of *me* running around?" She laughed. "The Lord knew exactly what He was doing when He molded each one of us uniquely."

Through her tears, Anna laughed. She lifted her pillow and grabbed her silk hankie. Daniel's hankie.

"My, that cloth has seen a lot of tears, hasn't it?"

Anna pressed it to her eyes. Only a hint of Daniel's comforting scent remained. "I'll be fine. Sorry."

"About?" Mary rested her cheek against her fist. "Everybody's got their own gifts, Anna."

"I know!" She sat up straighter. "I'll get used to the—"

"Ack!" Mary waved. "It's not the lizards, mosquitoes, and spiders." She laughed. "Big, big spiders, as you say."

"I love the children, Aunt Mary." Anna crushed the hankie tighter in her hand. "I really do."

"I know that, dear. But it's obvious you're not at peace. Keep seeking the Father's face. He'll give you the answers. Got it?" She stretched out, and pulled the covers over herself.

Anna nodded. "Yes, I got it." She snapped off the lamp on the nightstand, lay back, and stared into the darkness.

Seek the Father's face? Aunt Mary's words pricked her conscience and wouldn't let go. She had journeyed from New York to Haiti, leaving behind the love of her life to do the will of the Father. Was she a failure? Yes, she needed to pray for more strength. Her cushy life in the States hadn't prepared her to face these orphans—their hair orange and stomachs distended from malnutrition—or to see families living in mausoleums in the town graveyard.

Anna squeezed her eyes shut. *I can do this work, Lord. I'll be a good missionary. I will.*

But today she'd come close to packing her bags and running when that local man brought in two older kids he called *restavecs.* The elderly man with hollowed out cheeks explained the term. "Child slaves." He pointed to the young boy and called him "lucky." The girl beside him, a not-so-lucky teenager, had her finger chopped off as punishment by her owners.

Owners? Anna's stomach roiled. What if time proved she didn't have the strength to endure to the end? Alex, Darcy, Hope, Aunt Mary. . .*all* the missionaries here looked like they'd been born for the task.

Anna.

Anna jumped forward. Who called her name? "Yes?" Her gaze roamed the thick darkness. She held her breath, tilting her head to pick up sounds.

The pattern of Aunt Mary's breathing meant she was asleep. But the voice hadn't come from a woman.

Anna fell back against the pillow, strangely unafraid.

Anna, you are accepted. Not rejected.

The words came from deep inside, ringing through her spirit. Tears of joy stung her eyes. The still, small voice of the Father—*her* heavenly Father—piercing the walls to the inner, wounded part of her heart.

Silence pressed in. Anna watched with awe as in her mind's eye a vision appeared. Her heart, cleansed and healed, ascended from the center of a flower. Brown petals floated to the ground, swept away by a gust of wind. Love remained in its purest form. The love of the Father for *her*.

"Perfect love drives out fear." The words poured from Anna's mouth. She opened her eyes. The sun streamed into the window. *Is it morning?* She smiled. "Perfect love drives out fear." The Lord must have deposited the words in her mouth. Her mind hadn't engaged yet.

"Now you've got it!" Mary said.

Anna turned to see her aunt, kneeling beside a chair in the corner of the room, Bible open. Mary looked heavenward, smiling. "Thank you, Jesus."

❧

"Packages for Anna McCort!"

Anna turned from her spaghetti and ketchup breakfast. Alex ambled toward her, a box under each arm, his smile bright against his nutmeg skin. "And there are more outside, Anna."

"What?" She swung her legs over the picnic-style bench and took a few short strides to where Alex stood. She looked down at the boxes. "But I wasn't expecting anything."

Alex leaned over the carton, large hands on his kneecaps. "Return address says L-A-D in New York."

Some of the teachers and children gathered around. "Lad?" Anna shrugged. "Well then, let's open them."

Alex was ready with the box cutter as soon as the words left her lips. He made a quick slit down the center and flipped up the cardboard panels.

Anna gaped at the new, child-sized clothing. Amidst the chorus of *oohs* and *aahs*, she stooped to one knee and picked up a multicolored short set. "Who could've sent these?"

Two of the kids danced in circles, clapping their hands. "For us?" Rachael asked.

Anna smiled. "Yes, for you." She looked at the box panel to inspect the return address. "LAD International? A post office box in New York." She lifted her gaze to Hope. "I wonder if my church took up a collection."

"Look, Anna." Alex stood over one of the other open boxes. "There's an envelope in this one with your name on it."

"Oh, good!" She took it from Alex's outstretched hand. "How many more packages?" She inspected the ivory envelope, which bore only her first name, then returned her gaze to Alex.

"Ten boxes," Alex said, wiggling his fingers. He glanced heavenward. "Praise the Lord!"

"Oh, Anna, you have to see this!" Hope leaned over a box, her long, dark hair covering her face.

Anna laughed at the enthusiasm in Hope's usually serene voice. She slipped the envelope into the pocket of her sundress and hopped over an unopened carton.

Hope straightened. Anna's gaze went from the smile on

her rotund face to the bundle of various items she cradled in her arms.

Shaking her head, Anna picked out a baby bottle from the bundle. Pacifiers, lip balms, antiseptics. "I can't believe it. This is—"

"An answer to prayer." Hope finished the sentence for her.

"Yes, it is." Anna pressed her hand to her pocket, feeling for the envelope. "I think I'll go—" There was a tug at her dress. She looked down to find Hannah wearing her usual solemn face.

"I have this?" Hannah gestured to the lavender blouse in her hand.

"Sure. Let's try it on, okay?"

At Hannah's answering nod, she helped her slip the blouse over her T-shirt. A smile started on the little girl's face. Tears clouded Anna's vision. What a blessing the Lord had rained down on all of them this morning.

Hannah stepped back, head down, gazing up.

"You look adorable." Anna smiled. The blouse grazed Hannah's knees, but it seemed not to matter to her. Smiling, she skipped away and joined the other children.

Anna scanned the busy room. Children were everywhere examining the contents of the boxes and dancing in their new clothes. Their squeals and excited chattering filled her ears, and her heart. *Oh Lord, bless whoever has done this!*

Who *had* done this? Anna dipped her hand into her pocket and then backed into a chair in the corner. She opened the envelope and removed the matching ivory pages.

Dear Anna,
  How are you?

"Who is it from?"

Anna glanced up at Hope and then turned to the second page. Her gaze dropped to the signature on the bottom. Her heart thudded so wildly, the papers in her hand shook. She pressed her hands to her crossed knee and looked up. "A friend of mine in New York."

"What's your friend's name?" Alex stood by the door, his arms wrapped around a carton.

"Daniel." Anna smiled. "His name is Daniel."

"When you talk to Daniel"—Alex set the box down—"tell him we'll be praying for him."

When she talked to him? Her throat tightened. Chances were, she would never talk to Daniel again. "Thanks, Alex, I will."

At least she had his letter. Anna looked at the paper covered with bold pen strokes.

I spent a good deal of time at the Precious Children Web site and looked at the orphanage "wish list." I can see the children need everything. I called our downtown warehouse to start shipping clothes. Food and other items will arrive shortly. (By the way, LAD stands for Lucia, Antonio, and Daniel.) How do you like my mother getting top billing? As you once said, "She's got such a sweet, little voice." I'll say.

I imagine in the few weeks you've been there, the children have grown to love you. I saw the photos posted on the Web of the orphaned children. My prayer is that the Lord touches Christian hearts to want to adopt these kids. I also saw the picture you sent to church of Ryan, your four-year-old "sidekick" as you noted on the photo. Give Ryan and all the children hugs for me.

Anna turned to the next page, her hands still shaky. So far, his words hadn't revealed a shred of resentment toward her. She stared at the page. The backdrop of joy and laughter jabbed her with the reminder of what she'd lost.

Jane told me you're having difficulty adjusting to some of the creatures indigenous to the area. If it's any comfort, I sympathize with your fears. If I were there, I could do little more by way of rescuing you from bugs than holding you while you cringed.

Anna stopped for a breath. She'd been in his arms twice—once in Jay-Jay's, once for his kiss—and her only fear was that her heart might explode with all she felt for him. His arms around her would definitely suffice to chase away her bug phobia.

I hope you'll like the foods I'm sending. Please be sure to eat enough! You're in my prayers, Anna.

Love, Daniel

Anna folded the letter and tucked it back into the envelope. She stood and walked past the smiling children, most of them proudly donning their new clothes.

The sense of loss settled into a dull ache around her heart. Was this why the Lord had brought Daniel into her life? So Daniel would bless The Center, and now, these children? She leaned against the wall of the cafeteria, lifting her face to the sun. *Thank you, Lord, for blessing the children. Thank you for Daniel. You truly are a good and loving Father.*

Anna moved to the park bench, and looked at the envelope in her hand. He had written, *"Love, Daniel." Love.* Not that kind of *love*, of course, but his goodwill and thoughtfulness showed charity above and beyond what she could've dreamed.

By their fruit you will recognize them. She'd grown edgy in the limo, frustrated beyond reason discussing the verse with Daniel. Now, truth struck with startling clarity.

Anna pressed the envelope to her heart. She'd been afraid. . . terrified to acknowledge Daniel's acts of kindness as "good fruit." But her cynicism lost its lure too late.

"There you are!"

Anna jumped. "Oh, Aunt Mary. Have you seen the packages we—"

"Yes." Mary smiled. "I hear they're from your friend in New York." She sat beside her. "Would that be your Daniel?"

"Oh, he's not *mine*." Anna laughed without mirth. "But yes, they're from Daniel."

"There you have it." Mary rose abruptly. "Perfect love." She sprinted off.

Anna looked after her, then stood and started toward the schoolrooms. *Perfect love drives out fear.* Yesterday the verse lay dormant in her head. Today the words danced in her heart for the children.

"Hello, Miss Anna."

Anna pivoted. "Ryan!"

The happy-faced little boy ran toward her. Anna leaned down and scooped him into her arms. Ryan wrapped his skinny arms around her neck. "You take me home, Miss Anna? You be my mommy?"

"I'm here, Ryan. I'll stay here with you." Anna gave him a squeeze. "Why aren't you in class?"

"I must give something to Mr. Alex."

"I see." Anna walked into the classroom and deposited Ryan beside the other kids. Darcy looked up from the book she was reading to the children.

"Sorry to disturb, Darcy, but I'll be back in a little while."

Darcy waved her away. "No hurry."

Anna tiptoed out of the classroom and came to an abrupt halt. What did Daniel mean in the letter? *Hold her?* Maybe his gesture of goodwill went beyond helping the children. Her pulse quickened with hope. She hurried around the building to her room, pulling out the letter to read it again.

Anna flipped open the laptop and took a deep breath before flicking the ON switch. "Good!" For the moment, the electricity worked. She unsnapped the line from the phone and plugged it into the back of her computer, then pulled up a chair.

There! Everything was ready. Was she? She laid Daniel's letter on the dresser in front of her. "Give me the words, Lord. Please, give me the right words." On a deep breath she punched in her password to get online.

Dear Daniel,
   Thank you for the many packages you sent. I wish you

could've been here to see for yourself the joy you brought to the kids—and the adults! May the Lord bless you abundantly for your generosity.

So Jane "ratted" me out? (Pun intended.) Yes, I must confess to a deathly fear of bugs and rodents. However, there is hope. The Lord has been dealing with me about my fears, showing me how I've let fear triumph over faith in many parts of my life. Isn't it wonderful to know the Lord's always working in us and through us to shape us and mold us into His image? He doesn't hold our mistakes against us either.

Well, I must get back to the classroom. Thank you again, Daniel. I covet your prayers, and Alex, our local missionary, wants you to know we're all praying for you, as well. Have a blessed Christmas.

Love,
Anna

Anna hit SEND and snapped off the computer before she could give in to the temptation to reread what she'd written and then fret about double meanings.

twenty-six

After composing and deleting four e-mails, Daniel typed in "Dear Anna" again and stared at the screen. Now what? He scrubbed his hand across his jaw then stood.

He picked up the TV remote and severed the voice of the cheerful moderator harking in the New Year.

Happy New Year to me—and Happy Birthday. But he wasn't feeling happy at the moment.

Was he supposed to glean a deeper meaning from Anna's e-mail? She said God showed her that she had allowed fear to triumph over faith. Fear of him? Fear of what?

Daniel went to the desk and snapped off the computer. He refused to play cat-and-mouse games, wishful thinker that he was. Unless Anna gave him something concrete, he wouldn't set himself up for the pain of another rebuff.

Daniel dropped onto the sofa and clamped his hands behind his head. He shouldn't have been quick to turn down several New Year's Eve dinner invitations. Anna had started a new life without him. Maybe he should've spent the evening with family and friends.

He swiped off his tie and sat forward, his elbows resting on his knees. If he was dying on the inside in the privacy of his own apartment, watching couples holding hands, hugging, and kissing on TV, he'd be a thousand times worse off at a party.

Daniel closed his eyes. How had Anna made her way into his heart so deeply, so fast? He dragged his hands through his hair. "I know you can't hear me, Anna, but I love you. Happy New Year."

❧

Daniel stood in front of the bulletin board in the church's fellowship hall. Smiling, he tilted his head, examining the most recent photos Anna had sent from Precious Children.

"Hey, there."

Daniel turned. "Good morning, Brenda."

"So. . ." Brenda sighed. "Do you hear from her much?"

"Her name is Anna. And yes, I hear from Anna now and then." Daniel pointed to the photos. "She's busy doing God's work."

"She looks quite thin," Brenda said

Daniel held his tongue, though he'd noticed the same. At the sound of Brenda's departing footsteps, he shrugged, then zeroed in on the new photo of Anna holding her "sidekick."

She'd been gone nearly three months. He clasped his hands behind his back and drew a deep breath. And he'd been marking time since. Why couldn't he push her out of his mind?

She invaded his thoughts in the middle of board meetings, and she wiped smiles off his face when he entertained clients. Daniel closed his eyes. If he'd known his days with Anna were numbered, would he have done anything differently?

His gaze returned to Anna, cheek-to-cheek with Ryan. How long until the miracle—the day Anna would run into his arms where she belonged? Or the day he'd forget he ever met her?

He had everything. And he had nothing.

"Daniel Bee!"

Daniel smiled, recognizing Jane's voice before he turned to look at her. "Jane Roberts, what have you been up to?"

"Oh, this and that."

"Have you heard from Anna lately?" Daniel tried to keep his voice casual. But mentioning her name held a torment all its own.

"Yes. She's doing okay, I guess." Jane smiled. "I know she's truly touched by what you've been doing for the kids."

"Yes, she sent me a few e-mails." Nothing that told him Anna trusted him any more now than the day she walked out of his life. "Want some coffee?"

"Sounds great."

Daniel pulled out a chair for her. "Have a seat, and I'll bring it over." He walked to the coffee urn, picked up two cups, and began filling them. Everything reminded him of her. Maybe he should change churches. Maybe he needed a change of scenery.

Daniel returned to the table, set down the coffee cups, and sat.

"Thanks." Jane strummed her fingers on the table. "Why don't you go to Haiti?"

Daniel quirked a brow. "Try to understand. . ." His bruised heart came alive to taunt him. "Haiti is not the problem. People in love wait a lot longer than two years to be together."

"Don't you think I know that, Daniel?" Jane sipped her coffee. "Anna loves you, but maybe, she doesn't want to love you." She shrugged. "Know what I mean?"

Daniel stared into his cup. "Is that what Anna told you?" How easily hope flickered in his heart.

"Nooo, but I feel—"

"I see."

And how easily hope died.

Jane leaned forward. "No, you don't see. I'm telling you, Anna's heart is open. You. . .loving those kids the way you do, really caring. . . It's done something to her. I can read between the lines in her e-mails."

The pain was back, fresh, ripping out his heart. Daniel cleared his throat. "I spent time *misreading* between the lines with Anna. I may go to Haiti anyway."

Jane's eyes widened. "Daniel! Are you serious?" A smile started at her lips.

"Yes. Regardless of how Anna feels about me, the needs at the orphanage are great. I want to see for myself what I can do to help."

Jane sobered. "I am so proud of you."

Daniel crossed his arms. "And why is that?"

Jane sighed. "You're willing to put your feelings aside and put the children's needs first. That's awesome."

Daniel held up a hand. "I care deeply about the children and the ministry. I wish I were able to adopt all the kids myself. The other part? Putting my feelings aside?" He shook his head. "My heart is broken without Anna, but the thought of seeing her hurts even more. When I see her—"

"Hard to explain?" Jane frowned. "Gee, I hope a guy falls that madly in love with me someday."

Daniel laughed. "There you go, Jane. It's not very complicated. 'Madly in love.' I trip all over madly in love when I see Anna."

twenty-seven

Anna combed Emily's hair for the last time. "Your mommy and daddy are coming to get you today."

Emily smiled. Anna took her by the hand and led her to the full-length mirror.

"Look at you, Emily. You're beautiful."

Emily stopped sucking on her fingers. A smile lit her face. She smoothed her hands down her pink dress. "Thank you."

Daniel's gifts had brought more smiles than she could count. She'd have to write him an e-mail and scan a picture of Emily in the clothes he'd sent. Whatever happened to "Out of sight, out of mind?" She was the poster woman for "Absence makes the heart grow fonder." Four months, and her lovesick state had only deteriorated.

Anna went to the desk, opened the drawer, and grabbed her camera. "Sit over there, sweetheart."

The five-year-old flounced across the room and climbed up onto the chair.

"Fingers out of your mouth." Anna positioned the camera to include Emily's new clothes then snapped the photo. "Great!"

"Is Emily ready?"

Anna turned. "Are they here?"

Mary nodded. She put out her hand. "Come along, dear heart." Emily went to her. "Your new mommy and daddy are waiting."

Anna forced a smile. "A good-bye kiss, Emily?"

Mary released her hand. Emily walked forward hesitantly, her shy face partly hidden by her collar. "Bye-bye, Miss Anna."

Anna gathered her in a hug, closed her eyes, and pressed a kiss to her smooth cheek. "I love you, Emily."

Emily turned and took quick little steps toward Mary. She

stopped, glanced over her shoulder, and waved. "I love you, Miss Anna."

Tears surged to her eyes. Anna nodded. *I'll miss you, Emily.* She glanced around the empty playroom then moved to the window to watch the toddler depart with the Johnsons.

Joy and sorrow converged in her heart. The taste of tears met the smile tugging at her lips. *Thank you, Lord, for this loving couple.*

Anna turned from the window, went to the desk, and picked up her Bible. "Oh Lord, what else have you got in store for me today?"

❧

"E-mail, schmee-mail." Aunt Mary sprayed the mirror with glass cleaner. "Why don't you just call him?"

"Yeah." Anna restrained a smile. "Maybe I should." She glanced away from her aunt's reflection, ran the feather duster around the lamp, and cleared her throat. "The washing machines Daniel sent are such a blessing."

"They certainly are." Mary fanned herself with the cloth. "I've used the computer a few times to e-mail. Never did like it."

Anna laughed. "Everybody uses computers, Aunt Mary."

"Yep." Mary stuffed the rag and spray bottle into her apron pocket. She tilted her head. "But the human voice conveys so much more." She shrugged. "Just my opinion."

"Yes." Anna grabbed the mop handle. What would her voice convey? *I'm pathetic without you?* She pushed the mop back and forth under the bed. A movement from the corner of her eye raised the hairs on her arms. "Yikes!"

"Oh, dear." Mary came to her side, leaned forward, and laughed.

Anna drew back. "This is definitely the ugliest spider I've ever seen."

"I think the good Lord has taught you all the lessons you needed to learn. . .for now."

"What lessons?"

Mary dropped the cloth over the brown-black creature. "I'm

gonna let this one go free." With her fingers bunched around the moving lump under the rag, she scooped it up and went to the window.

Anna shuddered. "Oh, please!" She squinted, watching as Mary leaned over the sill and gave the cloth a shake. As her aunt walked toward her, Anna shuffled back. "Are you sure it's gone?" She eyed the cloth suspiciously.

Mary waved the rag around, then stuffed it back into her apron pocket. "Well, little niece, it's about that time."

"Now where are you going?"

"Me?" Mary shook her head. "I'm not going anywhere."

Anna glanced at her watch. "Am I supposed to be somewhere?"

"Yep, but I'll leave it to the Lord to tell you where." Mary strode out of the room.

Staring at the doorway, Anna tilted her head. She glanced at her watch again. "Where am I supposed to be, Lord?"

Anna finished mopping, sat on the bed, and lifted the phone. She set it down, then picked it up. Her throat tightened. Was this a desperate move? She shook her head. She wanted to thank Daniel for all he'd done for the kids. Since when had saying thank-you gone out of style?

With a stiff smile, she punched in the first three digits. "Wait a second." She hit the OFF button. "Better write it down." She opened the nightstand drawer and grabbed pen and notebook.

She put pen to paper, hands sweating, and began to write. *Hello, Daniel? It's Anna. Fine, fine. I just wanted to thank you for. . . Yes, I miss you, too.*

Anna dropped the pen and sighed. "What am I doing?" She tossed the book aside. On a deep breath, she grabbed the phone and punched in his number. The sound of one ring traveled to her ear. She held her breath. "He won't pick up," she whispered.

"Hello?"

"Hi—hi, Daniel!" Oh no! She sounded like that silly waitress, Kimberly.

"Yes?"

"It's me. . .Anna."

"Anna? Are you all right?"

"Yes, fine." Anna dragged her hand through her hair. "It's so hot here." A hideous laugh escaped her.

"Yes, I imagine."

"Anyway, I just wanted to thank you for the washing machines. We were scrubbing everything by hand, and we—"

"My pleasure."

Oh, just to hear his voice. . .the hint of his Italian accent. The roots of her hair tingled. She'd never get over him. Not in a million years. "Thanks so much."

"I received your e-mails thanking me."

"Did I write? About the washers?" Anna closed her eyes. Sweat trickled down her forehead.

"Anna. . .how are you doing? Is anything new?"

She wouldn't call being in love with him new. Anna squeezed her eyes closed. "Nothing too new. I'm busy, of course." She spun her hair tighter around her finger. "I've been teaching. . .under a leaky roof." She forced a laugh. "But, um, how about you?"

"No, nothing." A long silence hung between them. "I, um, thank you for calling me, Anna."

"Yes, you're welcome. So then, good-bye." Her knuckles whitened around the phone. She held her breath. A dial tone severed their connection.

"Knock, knock. I forgot my Bible."

Anna placed the phone in its cradle and turned.

"Uh-oh." Mary came to the side of the bed. "You had a rosy glow a couple of minutes ago, and now you look like death warmed over." She dropped to the edge of her own bed. "Make your call?"

Anna nodded. "I knew I should've stuck to e-mail, schmee-mail." She stared down at the worn floor. "I've lost the only man I'll ever love." She drew in a soft gasp. "There! I said it!"

"Maybe now that you're honest with yourself, you'll be honest with Daniel."

Anna gave a short laugh. "What? Call him back and say, 'Oh, I forgot to mention, I'm so in love with you I can't see straight'?" She shuddered. "Women don't do that."

Mary laughed. "Better read the story of Ruth and Boaz."

Anna's eyes widened.

"Oh, I'm not suggesting you sleep at the foot of Daniel's bed. That was Ruth's way of expressing her trust in Boaz to love her and care for her—and symbolic of how we're to trust in the Lord's love to care for us." Mary slapped herself on the thigh and laughed. "But, symbolic or not, the truth will set you free." She stood. "Got to get to my prayer meeting."

Anna stared after her aunt, then leaned back on the bed, and turned onto her side. Ruth and Boaz. Aunt Mary didn't get it. If there were phones back then, Boaz wouldn't have practically hung up on Ruth. And Ruth would've never stooped to playing on Boaz's sympathies.

She closed her eyes, praying for sleep. Her mind echoed with the phone conversation, replaying it word for word.

Anna abandoned the hope of respite through sleep and sat forward. "Tell him?" Why would Daniel trust her? She stood and swiped her Bible off the dresser.

Ruth was sweet and truthful. That's why Boaz loved her. No, she would never tell Daniel.

twenty-eight

The rain had stopped, but water still poured from a hole in the ceiling in a steady stream.

Anna hefted the overfilled bucket, sloshing water over her feet as she carried it to the door. She dropped it to the ground and tilted it with her foot.

"Hello there."

Anna looked up at Alex coming toward her. "Hi, what's doing?"

Alex swooped up the emptied bucket. "Your aunt said I should take over for you."

"What's wrong?" Anna followed him back into the classroom. He set the pail under the drip, then looked at her.

"Mary was called to the clinic to pick up a newborn." Alex pointed to the door. "She's expecting donors to arrive soon."

"Oh, I guess she wants me to show them around." Anna shrugged. "It's Bible-reading time for the kids."

Alex rubbed his hands together. "My favorite subject."

Anna smiled, started for the door, and turned. "Any idea where these contributors are from?"

"Florida?" Alex frowned. "Sorry, I forgot."

"No matter." Anna glanced at the sagging ceiling, sighed, and walked out the door. She strode toward the front of the building, pulling at the cotton dress that stuck to her skin. With a sigh, she dropped onto the park bench to await the bus. She tilted back her head, slowly breathing in the humid air.

Anna closed her eyes. *You know who these patrons are, Lord. Touch their hearts. Show them the many needs here.* She opened her eyes and watched a German shepherd–looking dog approach hesitantly. *Poor, abused mutt.* He looked too afraid to be happy.

"You know me by now, Mangy." Anna laughed. "Come on."

She dipped her hand into the pocket of her sundress. "Want to share a cookie?"

Panting, he skulked forward, sat, and looked up into her eyes.

Anna broke off a chunk of the cookie and tossed it to him. The rumble of the bus coming up the dirt road reached her ears.

Anna stood, hand outstretched. "You can have the rest."

Mangy lopped the cookie from her fingers in his first show of trust. "Good doggie."

The bus rounded the bend. Anna stepped back and squinted at the dusty windshield. Martin was driving. She waved.

The clunker groaned to a stop, and the doors opened. Martin gave her a bright smile. "Good afternoon."

"Afternoon, Martin."

Martin turned and looked toward the rear of the bus. "Need help back there?"

"No, thanks. I'm all right." The silky voice with the Italian accent echoed from the distance. The strength left Anna's limbs, and her heart thudded in her ears. Anna's smile disappeared. Only one voice. . .

Daniel came into view wearing khaki trousers, a white shirt, cuffed sleeves, his relaxed stance cool against the heat. He stooped, looked down at her, and nodded. "Anna."

She drew back, fighting to bring his name to her lips. "Daniel."

Martin spoke. Daniel responded. Their words spun around her head, as foreign to her as the Creole of the natives.

Daniel moved down the steps with nonchalance. The bus doors closed. The vehicle pulled away, leaving Daniel, in the flesh, standing in front of her.

He gazed into her eyes, unsmiling. "I suppose you're wondering what I'm doing here." He dropped his luggage at his side.

Anna smoothed her hands against her dress and tilted her chin. "Well, yes." The smile she summoned didn't come to her shocked face. She laced her trembling fingers lest her body, without her consent, rush forward into his strong arms.

Daniel clapped his hands behind his back. He looked over her head to a spot behind her. "I wanted to see for myself the extent of the damage." His dark gaze dropped to hers. "To determine what type of action I should take."

"Action?" A crackle of excitement zigzagged through her. "What kind of action?"

"When you mentioned the leaking roofs, I investigated further." Daniel quirked a brow. "Seems like there's a big project to be done here."

Anna nodded. He'd only gotten more irritatingly irresistible in four months. And he was here—not for her—but to investigate a construction project! She dabbed her forehead with the back of her hand.

Without taking his gaze off her, Daniel picked up his luggage and stepped forward. She remained stone still. "Would you mind showing me around?"

"Show you around? Yes, of course." Anna swallowed past the dryness in her throat. "It's so hot today, isn't it?" She pushed back the hairs sticking to her forehead.

"Heat doesn't bother me."

Anna blew out a breath. "Well, see now, that's really good." Fanning herself, she smiled. She strode up the walk ahead of him. She had no business reliving his kiss. He came here to check on leaky roofs, not the emotions leaking from her in an obvious puddle at his feet.

"You can leave your bag here." She indicated a spot under a sagging porch roof. "And we can get started in this building."

❧

Trailing Anna through the main building, Daniel kept his hands clasped behind his back. *Just one kiss. . .*

No. Even if she allowed him to hold her in his arms, reclaim her lips in a kiss, if he couldn't have her forever, the memory would only taunt him. He scanned Anna's golden hair, longer now, swaying angelically with her every step. He slipped his hands into his pockets.

Anna turned suddenly, colliding into his chest. Daniel stood, unflinching. Her turquoise gaze met his, crashed over him, lingered too long. She had to know. She had to see *I'm-crazy-in-love-with-you* written on his face.

⌘

With her eyes locked on his, Anna breathlessly reached behind her back and opened the door.

Daniel quirked a brow. A rush of heat seared her skin. Anna pivoted and strode across the nursery.

A smiling Darcy looked up and continued rocking an infant against her shoulder. "Darcy." Anna turned. "I'd like you to meet—"

"Daniel." Darcy stood, laughing. Clasping the baby with one arm, she offered her hand. "Anna, you described him very well."

Daniel turned to her and winked. Anna forced a smile. He shook Darcy's hand. "Pleased to meet you. Now, what did Anna say about me?"

The tawny-skinned woman laughed harder. "I cannot tell you." Daniel sucked his teeth. "That bad, huh?"

"No, no," Darcy said. "She say you look like a movie star. And she be right."

Anna straightened. "No, I only meant. . ."

Daniel grinned. "May I hold the baby?"

"Yes, of course." Darcy transferred the infant to his arms. "His name is Elisha."

Daniel kissed the top of the baby's head. "You have a great name, Elisha. It means God is my salvation."

Anna stared at him, Elisha against his chest. Her heart crushed with longing. She'd lost so much. In her stupidity, she'd misjudged him. She turned away and went to Alice's bedside. The toddler slept soundly. Anna ran her hand over her soft hair, then turned.

"The infirmary is down the hall if you'd like to go now." Daniel handed Elisha to Darcy. "Thank you, Darcy. The children are blessed to have you and Anna watching out for them."

"You are watching out for them, too." Darcy smiled.

Walking down the hall, Anna raked her mind for something to say. She stood beside the man she dreamed of day and night—the man she loved. But no words came.

"I'm glad I've come to see the orphanage for myself, Anna."

"Yes, me, too." Would he stay a few days? Would it make any difference? She stopped to open the door. "Wait." Daniel put his hand to her arm. "I'm happy, too, that I've had a chance to see you again. I want you to know that."

Did her ears pick up the sound of good-bye? Her heart pounded harder. Her face grew hot. She pushed open the door. "Hello, Hope, I'd like you to meet—"

"Daniel!" Hope strode across the room, hand outstretched.

Daniel smiled and shook her hand. "I'm feeling famous around here."

Hope smiled. "Thank you for all you're doing for the orphanage. God bless you." She turned her gaze on Anna. "Do you want to see Lydia? She's awake and talkative."

Anna nodded, but her stomach sank. The seventy-pound teen's worsening condition made seeing her an agony. She was about to explain Lydia's illness, but Daniel dropped to the chair beside the girl's cot.

Lydia smiled, causing her face to look more skeletal. She made several sounds in greeting. Daniel smiled and took hold of her bony hand.

"Lydia has AIDS," Hope whispered. "She's doing well today though."

Anna forced back the lump in her throat. "Hello, Lydia." She rarely entered the infirmary, and now she was reminded why. Her heart couldn't bear it. She had to force the tears to remain at bay for fear of upsetting the teen.

Lydia lifted her stick-thin arm in acknowledgment. Anna's eyes filled. "Maybe we should come back later?" She drew a breath and looked at the back of Daniel's dark head nodding.

"I'll come back to see you, Lydia." Daniel stood. "I promise."

Washing his hands at the sink, Daniel glanced her way.

"Right about now, I'd like to see Jesus in the flesh and weep on His shoulder."

Anna handed him a towel, then squirted soap into her hands. "Yes, I know." The sadness on his face mirrored the pain she'd been carrying in her heart for over four months. They were more alike than she wanted to believe—now that she couldn't have him. And oddly, their faces didn't reflect the hope and joy of the other missionaries.

ఌ

After a tour of the kitchen facilities, Daniel sat across the table from Mary and Anna. He put his spoon into the bowl of something that looked like cream of wheat. Whatever decision he made today would change the rest of his life.

"Look what I do, Miss Anna!" A little boy ran toward her and held his artwork about an inch from her face. Daniel smiled, recognizing him from the photos as her "sidekick."

"Wow!" Anna turned his picture this way and that. "You're some artist, Ryan." She squeezed his face and kissed him. "I'd like you to meet Mr. Daniel. He sent the paints and crayons."

Ryan peeped across the table, his broad smile revealing perfect teeth. "Thank you. I like these colors."

"Come here and let me see that picture." Daniel slid to the opening at the end of the bench. Ryan crawled up onto his lap, then held out his artwork with both hands.

Daniel looked from the picture to Ryan's expectant face. "I have a painting at home, but this is a masterpiece by comparison."

Ryan frowned. Anna and Mary laughed. "That means he really likes it, Ryan," Anna said.

Daniel squeezed him in a hug. Ryan set down the brown paper on the table. "This is for you."

Swallowing hard, Daniel smiled. "Thank you, Ryan. I'll cherish it forever." The toddler hugged him, then slipped off his lap and took off toward a group of children.

Daniel looked across the table. Anna lifted her gaze to him. Mary cleared her throat. "It's a blessing to meet you in person, Daniel. Any surprises?"

He nodded. "Yes, the love here is as enormous as the needs. But I realize my family won't be able to cover everything. I'll have to get friends and business associates involved in raising funds when I return to New York."

Anna dropped her spoon into her bowl and stood. "Would you both excuse me? I forgot to tell Alex about a delivery."

Daniel watched Anna dash toward the door and disappear. He switched his gaze to her aunt.

"You look concerned." Mary indicated the exit with her eyes. "Is something wrong?"

"I am concerned. . .about Anna." Daniel frowned. "She doesn't look very happy."

"I agree. You know, this ministry isn't for everybody." Mary's smile disappeared. "In fact, I'm sorry if I somehow persuaded Anna that she needed to follow in my footsteps." She pushed her bowl aside and looked him in the eye. "Anna is tenderhearted. She wants to help, but it's tearing her up. She's having a tough time adjusting to the hardships, although she never complains." Mary shrugged. "We're not all born to be single missionaries."

"No, but this is what Anna wants." Daniel examined the woman's wizened face. A hint of humor danced in her eyes. "Isn't it?"

"Is it?" Mary shrugged. "Are you afraid to ask her?"

"Perhaps. I don't—"

"Want to influence her to leave?" Mary smiled broadly. "Let the Lord go worrying about things like that. The truth will set you free."

Daniel sighed and nodded. How deep would a second rejection cut? "Who could argue with truth?" The Lord called His followers to be honest—regardless of the anticipated response. Still. . .

He had no right to question Anna's calling.

twenty-nine

Daniel punched the pillow and tucked his hands behind his head. He stared at the ceiling in the darkened hotel room.

He would've been willing to sleep in what Mary had referred to as "slave's quarters"—a room like the one she and Anna shared in back of the orphanage. But they'd all insisted he would get a better night's rest with the conveniences at the hotel.

Rest? Images of Anna filled his mind.

"Lord, did I hear You wrong? Was it for the sake of the children only that You told me to come here?"

The thought slammed into his chest and clutched his heart. If she loved him, even if God wanted to send Anna home, would she ever allow herself the grace to go? Daniel blew out a breath. Whatever flicker of encouragement Mary's words sparked in him had been quickly extinguished in Anna's reserved presence.

"Tomorrow, Lord." Daniel turned onto his side. "Tomorrow, the truth will set me free and maybe tear out my heart in the process."

❧

"You haven't been to the reading room or the playroom yet. Would you like to see them?"

"Yes." Daniel prayed as he followed Anna down the hall. Stepping into the ring could result in another knockdown blow. This time the damage would be more devastating than the first. He clasped his hands behind his back, admiring her bare sun-kissed arms.

They arrived at a door with a paper sign that read "Reading Room." With her gaze on him, Anna reached behind her back and jiggled the knob. "It's not. . .open."

Daniel tilted his head, measuring her uncertain smile.

163

"Hmm, where should we go from here?" He left the words hanging between them, pregnant with double meaning.

Anna sighed. "I—we. . ."

He brushed her hair away from her forehead, then traced his fingers slowly down the side of her face to the hollow of her neck. "I've missed you, Anna."

Anna sank against the door and closed her eyes. "I–I've missed you, too." Color flamed across her cheeks.

Daniel's resistance crumbled. He slipped his hand behind her neck and drew her forward. "You're so beautiful."

Her eyes glistened. A smile tipped the corners of her sweet lips.

He leaned down, trailing kisses along her face to her soft mouth. The gentle pressure of her hands against his chest made him stop.

"Wait." Anna's hands slid down his arms. She held his hands. "I have to tell you something, Daniel." Her warm breath feathered against his mouth. Her words carried a pain that brought him to his senses. He drew a breath. "Don't say anything."

Her fragile hands gripped his tighter. "I have to."

Daniel nodded, feeling the tremor in her fingers. He could wait another minute. "I suppose you do."

"I'm sorry." She took a deep breath. "I should've told you from the start that I was coming to Haiti. And I should've told you that"—slipping her arms around his waist, she rested her face against his chest—"I love you, Daniel." The moisture from her breath warmed his shirt. She looked up into his eyes. "I've loved you from the first time we spoke."

Joy flashed through him. He cupped her face, kissed her soundly, then raised his arms to the heavens and let joy explode from him in a burst of laughter. "She loves me, Lord! Glory, hallelujah, she loves me!"

He clasped her arms and gave her a little shake. "Are you sure?"

Anna laughed, nodding. Tears filled her eyes.

Daniel drew her against his chest. "You've always loved me?" He pulled back and looked into her eyes. "You drove me crazy, Anna McCort. I've been miserable without you. I've loved you from the moment I saw you." He stroked her hair. "Now, what are we going to do about this?"

Leaning back, Anna looked at him. "We need to talk—"

Daniel searched the depths of her eyes. "You won't have to leave Haiti. I've learned that I have to put hands and feet to my faith. We can stay here and do God's work together."

Anna ran her hand down his face. "I've learned a lot, too, Daniel. I was wrong not to recognize the value of the gifts the Lord has given you. I came and washed the children's clothes by hand; you sent washers to do the work of dozens of hands." She smiled. "I believe in my heart we'll be more valuable to the orphanage if we go home to New York."

"Home?" Daniel smiled. "I never thought I'd live to hear you call New York *home*." He pressed his forehead to hers. "I feel the same way, but I would've never asked you to leave. We can work together in New York." He searched his pocket, took out the ring, and hid it in his cupped hand. "We'll spread the word about the needs here—about the orphans."

Anna tousled his hair with her fingers. "This is real, isn't it? Tell me I'm not dreaming."

"Proof." Daniel dropped to one knee, took her hand, and looked up. "I'll love you always. Will you be my wife, Anna McCort?"

Nodding, she bit her lip. "Yes, I will." Tears slid down her face.

He slipped the ring on her finger and stood. "I meant to give you this on your birthday, but the Lord's timing is perfect."

"It's so beautiful." Anna closed her eyes. "I love. . ." It was as far as she got. Daniel's patience ran out. He crushed her to himself, lowered his head, and covered her lips with his.

❧

Sitting on the park bench in front of the orphanage, Anna could scarcely believe two weeks had passed since Daniel proposed.

"I can't complain, Aunt Mary. Tomorrow, I marry the man of my dreams." She shrugged. "I couldn't expect people to drop whatever they were doing to attend our wedding on such short notice."

"At least your mom and dad will be here. How kind of Daniel to pay their expenses."

"Yes, he's very generous." Anna lifted her face to the breeze rustling through the trees. Her love for Daniel overflowed her heart, spilling into every vessel and pore of her being. She might burst for the joy inside her.

"Daniel's parents will be here, too." Mary sighed. "But I would love to have seen Adam and Lynn again. I bet your nephews have grown some."

"Yes, I'm sure I wouldn't recognize them." Anna smiled. "And Jane. You would've loved meeting her. She's so funny."

Mary laughed. "I've gathered from some of the stories you've told me."

"Oh, and Daniel's cousin, Nicole—she's a character." Anna laughed. "Well, Alex borrowed a video camera from a friend. I'll send everyone a tape."

Mary nudged her. "Can you envision your knight in shining armor wearing a tuxedo?" She fanned herself.

Anna's eyes widened.

Mary laughed. "Now, just because I'm single and a missionary doesn't mean I don't recognize drop-dead handsome when I see it."

"Aunt Mary!" Anna burst into laughter.

"Seriously, little niece. But more than that, you're perfect for one another." Mary tapped her chest. "I feel it in here."

"Yes, so do I." She wanted to look perfect for Daniel tomorrow. "Do you like my dress?"

"Yep. It's a miracle we found anything on such short notice. Are *you* happy with it?"

Anna managed a smile. "It's fine." She stood. "I guess I'll change before the bus gets here."

"Good idea." Mary stood. "But make sure you're in the

cafeteria by two thirty. We'll have lunch with the families."

"Will do." Anna walked to the rear of the orphanage, entered her room and closed the door. Clasping her hands in front of her, she practiced her step-and-pause wedding walk as she made her way to the closet.

A happy sigh escaped her as she studied her wedding gown hanging on the door. Who cared what her dress looked like? She was about to become Mrs. Boccini. She removed the plastic bag and smiled, her heart lifting as she imagined her beloved's face as she walked down the aisle to become his wife.

Anna lifted the bottom of the skirt in an attempt to fluff it up. "Oh, well." They'd done their best turning the town upside down to find a dress. She should be happy the secondhand shop carried anything at all.

Anna pulled her robe from the closet. She stopped in front of the dresser mirror. Maybe with the right makeup? She lifted her hair off her neck.

At the rap on the door, she let her hair fall. "Who is it?"

"Hope."

"Oh." She swung open the door.

Smiling, Hope indicated the box at her side. "This is for you."

Anna moved back. "That's odd." Hope dragged it in by the wooden handle attached to the twine. "I wonder why it's coming to my room." With Hope's help, they lifted it onto the bed.

"Daniel said this belongs to you."

"Daniel?" Anna retrieved scissors from the pencil cup on the dresser. "Let's see what's in it."

Hope laughed. "I'll stay then."

"Yes, of course." She cut the cords then pulled up the lid and peeled back the pink tissue paper. "Ohhhh!" Anna lifted the white silk and lace gown from the box, tears burning her eyes. "But how. . ."

Hope pressed her hands to her round face. "Anna, Anna. I never saw anything more beautiful in all my life."

After Hope left, Anna showered and changed into her new sundress. She brushed back her still damp hair and hurried out of her room to the cafeteria. She couldn't wait to see her parents! She couldn't wait to see Daniel! Tomorrow she would look like a princess for him. How did he know the perfect fit? The perfect dress? *Oh Father, You've blessed me beyond words.*

Anna entered the cafeteria and ran, smiling, toward the table where her parents and Daniel's parents sat with Aunt Mary. They all rose as one.

"Daddy!" Simultaneously they flung their arms around one another. Anna laughed and cried into his shoulder. "And, Mom!" Anna cried, as her mother joined their circle of hugs and kisses.

"We've missed you so much," they kept repeating.

"I've missed you, too." Anna brushed away her tears. "Did you have a good flight?"

They nodded as Lucia and Antonio greeted her with laughter, kisses, and embraces.

Pausing for breath, Anna finally sat between her parents. "Where's Daniel? Have you met Daniel yet?"

Her father put his arm around her. "We have, and we heartily approve of your choice."

"Yes, we do." Her mother squeezed her hand. "We'll be proud to call Daniel our son-in-law."

Suddenly, hands covered her eyes. "Guess who?"

"Hmm, I don't know, but you smell delicious." Anna clapped her hands over his. "Are you tall, dark, and handsome?"

Daniel dropped his hands to her shoulders. Anna turned to him. "Daniel, the gown. . ." She stood, falling snugly into his embrace. Leaning back, her gaze went to the movement in the corner of the room. Her breath caught. "Jane!"

Jane screamed, and Daniel moved aside, laughing. Anna spread her arms and ran toward her friend. They hugged so hard, she thought they might tip over with joy. "I thought you couldn't make it."

"Didn't Daniel tell you?" Jane shot a glance his way. "He flew all of us in." She wore her sly grin.

"I knew he flew my parents in, but. . ." She turned and

rushed to him. "Oh, Daniel, thank you."

"My pleasure." He winked. "But I feel like I'm forgetting something."

"Forgetting what?"

Jane frowned. "That's funny; I've got the same feeling."

"Aha!" Daniel sucked his teeth. "The surprise in the kitchen." He grabbed her hand. "Come on."

Anna ran beside him but stopped short before entering the door. "It's not our wedding cake, is it? I don't want to see the cake before—"

Daniel smiled and opened the door. A chorus of "surprise" filled her ears.

Anna gaped at the cluster of people filling the small room. Lynn converged on her first. Her husband, Peter, came from behind a counter with the boys. Anna hugged him, then dropped to her knees and planted kisses atop her nephews' blond heads. Nicole swooped around her, grabbed her shoulders, and kissed her on the cheek. And then, there was Adam.

Anna threw herself into her brother's arms, laughing. He squeezed her so hard she was sure she heard her rib crack. "That's quite a guy you snagged for yourself, Sis." He cleared the thickness in his voice and grinned down at her. "I've a feeling birthdays and holidays for you are never going to be the same." He gave her another crushing hug. "Now, let's go eat. I'm starved!"

thirty

Aunt Mary stepped up to the dais, which Alex had constructed for their special day. She opened her Bible, smiling. "I'm honored to give a blessing to this couple." Mary cleared her throat. "And as much as I love them, it's about time these two lovebirds flew the coop."

Everybody laughed. Mary shook her head. "I'll keep this short and sweet. I quote from the book of John 21:15. The Lord asked, 'Do you truly love me more than these?' And I know for certain that Anna and Daniel have responded, 'Yes, Lord.'"

Mary's eyes filled. "In asking this couple to leave their worldly treasures behind, the Lord tested their faith." She sniffled. "And as you can see, God's blessings to them are priceless."

⁊⁊

Anna walked to the altar, gripping the hodgepodge bouquet of local flowers the children at the orphanage had picked for her. A hush fell over family and friends sitting in folding chairs at the outdoor ceremony. Her father lifted her veil, kissed her cheek, then shook Daniel's hand. Her mom gave her a tearful wave.

Anna's voice trembled with happiness as she spoke her vows. Oh, how she loved this man the Lord had chosen for her. Her eyes filled as Daniel pledged his undying love and slipped the wedding ring on her finger. And then, when she thought it was over, he looked into her eyes and said, "There's one more thing. . ."

Anna shivered as her husband took her hands. She caught her breath at the love for her that blazed in his eyes. He gave her a reassuring smile. " 'This is now bone of my bones and flesh of my flesh; she shall be called "woman," for she was taken out of man.'"

At last, she heard the words she longed to hear from the only man she ever wanted to say them. Joy washed through her. She stood on tiptoes and kissed Daniel's soft, welcoming lips to the applause of the congregation.

epilogue

Anna unfastened her seat belt. *Don't be late, Daniel.* Almost time for takeoff. She glanced at her watch. He should have had plenty of time after his meeting to make it to JFK.

She gripped the armrests, raised herself, and peered up front. A smile tugged at her mouth. She'd never get over the sight of him entering a room. Not in a million years.

Daniel made his way up the plane aisle, stopped, and clicked open the compartment above her head.

Anna coughed. "Hi, handsome."

Daniel snapped the compartment closed and dropped his gaze to her.

She tapped the seat. "Want to sit next to me?"

Daniel quirked a brow. "Hmm, I don't know, I. . ."

"I promise." Anna restrained a grin. "I won't bite."

Daniel sighed and dropped into the seat beside her. He gave her a sideways glance. "What's your name?"

"Anna Boccini." She put out her hand in a motion to shake his. "And yours?"

The man across the aisle leaned forward in rapt attention.

"Daniel." He kissed her hand.

Anna leaned close to his ear. "You smell delicious, Daniel."

A hint of a smile reached his eyes. He turned and pulled her to him in a kiss. "I love you. And I have a present for you later."

"A present?" Anna's eyes widened. "What's the occasion *this* time?"

"Our nine-month anniversary." He slid his gaze to her. "But, of course, you remembered."

"Oh, Daniel, now I feel guilty."

"Good. I've got you exactly where I want you."

Anna laughed. "Nine months." She nuzzled her head against his shoulder. The days since their wedding had passed so quickly.

"Who would've thought you'd like living in Manhattan?" Daniel squeezed her hand. "The Lord taught us so much."

"Yes, He did." Anna's eyes teared. And today, God would add even more blessings to their lives.

ꝛ

Standing in back of the orphanage, Daniel gripped Anna around her waist. "I can't wait to see him again."

"Me, too." Anna hugged him tighter. "This is like a dream, Daniel. God is awesome."

"*Shh*. I hear them."

"Who wants to see me Miss Mary?" Ryan's voice echoed through the passageway. Anna and Daniel exchanged glances.

"It's a surprise," Mary said. "If I tell you, it won't be a surprise."

Mary and Ryan rounded the corner and came into view.

The toddler's big brown eyes widened. A smile broke out on his face. "Miss Anna!" He jerked his hand from Mary's and raced forward, laughing.

Anna and Daniel stooped and caught him in their arms. They huddled together, hugging and kissing.

"Be back later." Mary walked away.

Daniel laughed. "Not 'Miss Anna,' Ryan. From now on she's Mommy."

"Mommy?" Ryan spun around clapping. He stopped, hugged Anna, and then looked at Daniel. "You be my daddy? I go home with you?"

Daniel nodded. "You'll come home to New York with us, Ryan. We love you so much."

They stood, Anna swiping tears off her cheeks. "Ryan, do you think you'd be a good big brother?"

Ryan bobbed his head.

"Good." Anna drew a breath and met Daniel's gaze. He stared back at her, his eyes full of questions.

"Anna? What are you—"

"I was afraid you wouldn't let me travel if I told you. But. . ." Anna flattened her hand over her stomach.

Daniel's wonder-filled gaze took Anna's breath away. She went wordlessly into his arms, and together they wept their gratefulness to God.

"I promise, I be a good big brother."

They glanced down to find Ryan looking up with a mix of adoration and apprehension on his face. Anna's heart went out to him. She nodded to Daniel, and he scooped their son into his arms.

"I know you will, son. You'll be the best big brother any baby ever had." He turned to Anna, his eyes still damp. "Let's go home, my love."